Co~~n~~
Confidential

Can a family survive the pressures of lockdown?

One woman's struggle to salvage relationships within it and heal the trauma of the past

Susana Cory-Wright

Copyright © 2020 Susana Cory-Wright

All rights reserved.

ISBN: 9798663946445

For all those for whom lockdown has not presented the opportunity to learn another language, take up embroidery, bake sourdough and be Zoomed within an inch of their lives but rather, have felt alone and ignored; for whom day to day survival has been all-consuming

And with love for the real 'Les Girls': Arabella, Catriona, Debbie, Fatima and Polly - 40 years to the day since we left Woldingham - I couldn't have got through this without you

In memory of Tim Pride 1965 - 2020

ACKNOWLEDGMENTS

Tolstoy's maxim that 'Happy families are all alike; unhappy families are unhappy in their own way' was never so true given the recent experience of lockdown. This period of isolation has come to mean different things to different people. For many, it came as a thunderous bolt from the blue, for others it was expected. What cannot be denied, is that Covid-19 has impacted us all. There has been considerable suffering and many people have lost loved ones.

I want to thank the teachers of The Pilgrims' School, who in so many instances went far and beyond the call of duty to ensure the wellbeing of their pupils. I wish also to salute the many unrecorded acts of kindness we must all have witnessed at some time or other, during this remarkable time.

But more immediately, I want to thank my husband Jonathan who kept our spirits up and our bellies full enticing us with ever more delectable dishes - the extra pounds are on you. And as ever, my love goes to my wonderful children - Emma, James and Maximilian. Without you, my darlings, nothing is possible.

Corona Confidential

The Great Realisation

"Tell me the one about the virus again, then I'll go to bed."
"But, my boy, you're growing weary, sleepy thoughts about your head."
"That one's my favourite. Please, I promise, just once more."
"Okay, snuggle down, my boy, but I know you all too well.
This story starts before then in a world I once would dwell.
It was a world of waste and wonder, of poverty and plenty,
Back before we understood why hindsight's 2020
You see, the people came up with companies to trade across all lands
But they swelled and got much bigger than we ever could have planned
We always had our wants, but now, it got so quick
You could have anything you dreamed of, in a day and with a click
We noticed families had stopped talking, that's not to say they never spoke
But the meaning must have melted and the work life balance broke
And the children's eyes grew squarer and every toddler had a phone
They filtered out the imperfections, but amidst the noise, they felt alone.
And every day the skies grew thicker, 'till you couldn't see the stars,
So, we flew in planes to find them, while down below we filled our cars.
We drove around all day in circles, we'd forgotten how to run
We swapped the grass for tarmac, shrunk the parks 'till there were none
We filled the sea with plastic because our waste was never capped
Until, each day when you went fishing, you'd pull them out already wrapped
And while we drank and smoked and gambled, our leaders taught us why
It's best to not upset the lobbies, more convenient to die
But then in 2020, a new virus came our way,
The governments reacted and told us all to hide away
But while we were all hidden, amidst the fear and all the while,
The people dusted off their instincts, they remembered how to smile
They started clapping to say thank you and calling up their mums
And while the car keys gathered dust, they would look forward to their runs
And with the skies less full of voyagers, the earth began to breathe
And the beaches bore new wildlife that scuttled off into the seas
Some people started dancing, some were singing, some were baking
We'd grown so used to bad news, but some good news was in the making
And so when we found the cure and were allowed to go outside
We all preferred the world we found to the one we'd left behind
Old habits became extinct and they made the way for the new
And every simple act of kindness was now given its due."
"But why did it take us so long to bring the people back together?" "Well
sometimes you've got to get sick, my boy, before you start feeling better
Now, lie down and dream of tomorrow and all the things that we can do
And who knows, if you dream hard enough, maybe some of them will come true
We now call it The Great Realisation and yes, since then, there have been many
But that's the story of how it started and why hindsight's 2020."

Tom Roberts

Corona Confidential

Corona Confidential

Corona Confidential

1

The very morning their Avianca flight landed at London's Heathrow Terminal 5, Boris Johnson announced a partial lockdown. Carla was relieved to be returning - the trip home had been as indirect as it was possible to be but not because of the 'virus'. Their flight originating in Cartagena had stopped in Bogotá, El Salvador and Newark before embarking on its final leg. That was only the way back - the outward journey had been even more complicated. But she was glad things had worked out the way they had. They could have flown directly from Bogotá to Madrid (as Seb regularly reminded her during their tedious six hour-lay over in the States) which would only have involved one change, but that would have meant flying Iberia. Inexplicably, Carla had taken a loathing to that airline. She considered its Spanish flight attendants too haughty - service was certainly accompanied with a disdainful snarl, a curl of the lip as if to say, 'This is not my real job - I'm of course a physicist, neurologist' (whatever) - 'in my spare time.' No, give her good old British Airways any day, even if the old dollies were heading towards retirement - more Mumsie than Miss Singaporean-nubile.

As it turned out, had they chosen that option, they'd have been stranded in Madrid. Spain had reported thousands of cases and a hundred daily deaths from a virus that would soon become a household word. Meanwhile, flights were turning around mid-air as the entire country closed down. They'd heard rumbles while they were away - well she'd dismissed them as rumbles, Seb was avidly following the news - his phone interrupting their conversation with regular updates. She had to admit to being a little surprised at the number of non-Asians wearing masks, homemade or otherwise - sometimes they just wore scarves around their faces.

Seb had expressed amazement at hers. "What do you mean you're surprised?"

"Well, they're not ... *Japanese*, are they?" Carla was used to seeing Japanese tourists running around Winchester, looking as though they were about to assist with open-heart surgery. And rubber gloves - those were everywhere. If she was surprised at seeing masks, rubber gloves when wielded by airport staff *always* made her nervous, causing her to clench her buttocks tight. If that wasn't enough, calls on the tannoy asked any travellers recently returned from China, France or Spain to 'make themselves known.' By the time they'd reached San Salvador, the list had included Panama.

"Do you think they mean capital or country?" whispered Seb. She could feel him mulling over the difference - weighing up the implications of answering honestly.

As his hand began an upwards trajectory, Carla slapped it down quickly. "Mind my bag, will you?" she said to distract him while she went to the loo. By the time they wheeled their carry-on luggage through UK customs, she had to concede that the rumbles had become something significantly more.

They'd argued for hours in the run-up to their departure. To begin with, all this recent talk about a 'virus' amused Carla. Her Spanish father had been sickening for one (in his case pronounced 'beeruus') for years. It always overcame him when her mother (his wife) expected him to attend social events he didn't want to, carry out any house improvements (he'd never so much as held a hammer) babysit (especially his own children) and every Christmas Eve without exception. But neither did death alarm her. Reared in an Hispanic family, she had inherited its slightly morbid fascination with the subject. They talked a great deal about death: good deaths and painful ones - there was a consensus that the more you suffered, the more of a *Cristiano* you were. There were violent deaths, ghoulish deaths, unexpected deaths, tragic deaths (those taken too young or those that left one partner pining for the other) and of course, near-deaths. Carla liked those best of all - where life, not its counterpart, was the outcome.

Carla's all-time favourite, however, combined a near-death with a murder and it concerned an acquaintance of her grandfather's. This gifted lawyer who had graduated top of his class had also schemed to kill his pregnant wife. Carla never knew the motive. He'd laced his wife's orange juice with poison, but by some fluke, their three-year-old daughter had drunk it instead. The child had died, his wife had become very ill but survived and the lawyer, her grandfather's friend, had gone to prison. His wife visited him every day during the long years of his imprisonment, met him when he was finally released and together they retired to the Balearic Islands where they'd set up a hotel and lived out the rest of their days in perfect harmony. The overriding anxiety of her grandparents' later years was that they would leave their affairs in order when the time came for them to die and that there would be a priest on hand to hear a final confession. But then fear affected people in different ways. Seb was happy to play in a sport where death stalked every game and yet was terrified at the prospect of catching a chill. He was especially worried that the woman who had sat behind them on their flight to Cartagena de Indias was infected.

"Ten days," Seb muttered. "Ten days and we'll know whether we've got it - whether *I've* got it. Of course, if I get it,

I'm dead."

"Don't be ridiculous - why should you get it?" she'd said through gritted teeth. It was a conversation they'd repeated countless times since the first news flash came through. "Why are you any more likely to get it than me?"

"I was hospitalised for pneumonia."

"Yes," she replied patiently. "Once. Twelve years ago. You've not been ill since."

"I'm almost seventy."

"You're fifty-eight."

And yet this new fear, this incredible, soon-to-be reality-fear, this contagion (clearly much more than a 'beeruus') for which the world was so ill-prepared, was fast becoming a reality. It might have been Carla's imagination, but did everything feel eerier? It was early, but in the time that it had taken to walk across the tarmac, hundreds of flights had been cancelled. Heathrow felt the same, and yet not the same. Shockingly, in the two weeks since they'd been away, the world as they knew it was irrevocably changed. They were still unaware by just how much.

Carla left Seb to wait for his luggage. She never checked hers, never trusting baggage handlers not to completely maul her expensive, recycled-American imports nor risk its designer content being nicked somewhere along the journey from check-in to arrival. A friend of hers had had a Chanel 2.55 (black caviar leather) and knitted dress stolen from her boyfriend's hand luggage when they travelled to Miami. Carla wasn't going to let that happen. Besides, she never dressed for comfort - sneakers, joggers were anathema to her.

After several goes, she had perfected the art of the capsule wardrobe for long haul. For the journey home, she had opted for stone Max Mara Capris, a black Pucci blazer and Prada slides from the SS 2019 collection. Smugly, she pushed her durable recycled polycarbonate bag on its smooth, double spinner wheels through the sliding doors.

"Carbon steel bearings?" Seb had scoffed. "Aircraft-grade aluminium handle? *Vegan* leather detail? *Really?*"

Well, who was laughing now? she thought priggishly. Here she was, ready to grab the shuttle bus to collect their car from Purple Parking, and there was Seb gnawing his thumbnail, pulling at his still crazily long hair, winding himself up into a frenzy of increasing dread. God he still looks good, she thought dispassionately as she whisked through the empty aisles of T5's M&S selecting a carton of semi-whole milk, bananas and a loaf of bread. They'd have porridge when they got home. She had to admit Seb's porridge was second to none.

She grabbed a newspaper and almost dropped the contents of her shopping bag. *Banks act to save economy from pandemic* declared one, while *The Times'* headline: *PM tries to regain grip as death toll rises* trickled a pinprick of disbelief. *Death* toll? Not in England, surely? This had to be an exaggeration? A few older people getting the flu wasn't anything to be alarmed about, was it? She dropped her shopping into a wire basket pushing the Aviator luggage to one side and rummaged through the other dailies. There was something wrong about *The Guardian's* front page. At first, she couldn't work it out and then she realised that the image depicted The Pope blessing a completely *deserted* St Peter's square. The accompanying column read: *Europe puts 100m on lockdown as toll grows.*

"Stay safe," piped the check-out girl. She was wearing a mask and rubber gloves. But then she *was* Asian. Carla muttered something unintelligible in reply. Rumblings of hunger, coupled with the movement she still felt of the plane, and this surreal situation were beginning to make her feel odd. Carla shivered, clutching the pint of slightly leaking milk. Suddenly she was impatient. Why couldn't Seb be better organised? They'd be out of Customs by now together if he had. Hunger was making her tetchy. She refused to spend another minute fretting about the unknowable other. Propping her M&S bag on top of her luggage, she glided from the shop down the empty arrivals lounge. Seb was through, after all, head buried in his phone.

"OK?"

"Yup."

"Excited about seeing the boy?"

Carla didn't have to hesitate.

"Always."

They sat in silence speeding along the M3, listening to alarming reports about the spread of the mystery virus - something some people in some countries were likening to a pandemic. The news seemed incredible, improbable. They, on the other hand, seemed untouchable - fresh (well they had been a few days earlier), tanned and fit from a lovely holiday. All that was in Carla's mind was getting home, unpacking and seeing Alfie that evening at 6 p.m. when his official exeat began. She forced her mind into neutral. Seb's, on the other hand, was churning. She could almost *hear* the integrative fibres of the prefrontal cortex neurons spinning towards the emotional structures of his brain. When her phone pinged a few moments later, she was surprised Seb couldn't hear hers. The mother of a Spanish boy, a classmate of Alfie's who shared a dormitory with him, texted asking whether he could stay with her. *Why not at school?* Carla tried to be friendly, but this was definitely breaking the holiday glow spell. *Because it's looking for guidance in case of quarantine.*

Quarantine?

"Do you think we should go into quarantine?" said Seb as though reading her thoughts.

Carla stared at him. It was uncanny the way he did that as if he really could. Or else he'd glanced down and seen her text. She looked away, dropped her phone onto the floor of the car, pushing it to one side with her foot and forced herself to remain calm. "Why would we want to do that?"

A car beeped him as they drifted into the slow lane. Seb didn't like to make a big thing about indicating. Instinctively her whole body shifted forward as though straining for the clutch.

"Because we've been travelling so much recently? They're saying we should probably self-isolate and given the woman on the plane-"

"You aren't serious."

"Why wouldn't I be?" Seb's tone had taken on an edge. The kind it did when they were about to fight. "I'm in the high-risk category," he explained patiently. "Will you self-isolate with me?"

Carla felt every nerve begin to tingle. "Can we talk about this later?"

"No, I want to know now. I *need* to know if you will."

Carla took a breath. "So, what do you mean by it - this 'isolation' thing - exactly?" She knew she was stalling, but she also knew Seb well enough to know that a non-committal answer wouldn't be enough.

"I mean -" his voice rose, trying to make himself heard over Radio 3.

She fiddled with the knob turning down the volume, a curtain of her hair hiding her face.

"*It* means we don't go out for two weeks - we don't see anyone."

"We can't *not* see people!" she said irritation getting the better of her. "Besides, Alfie's coming home. He'll want to see his friends. Just before his big exams, he'll *need* to."

Seb considered this, accelerated when they weren't talking, significantly slowing down when they were.

"True," he conceded, mentally calculating the risk. "OK then, after he's gone back Monday."

Carla did a mental calculation of her own. Her stomach was rumbling now - giant unhappy growls.

He looked at her waiting for an answer. She motioned to the cars ahead, indicating that he should keep his eyes on the road, but she knew he was capable of staring at her until she replied. "Well?"

"No." But because she'd said it with a smile he misunderstood.

"Excellent."

There was a brief, companionable silence. Happy now, Seb began texting with one hand, the other lightly steering. Given that they'd already shared one near-fatal accident she was amazed at his nerve (or irresponsibility). She'd become a jumpy passenger as a result, but her edginess was contagious.

"Don't do that!" he snapped. "I saw him," he added. "Have I *ever* had an accident?"

The implication that it was Carla who'd caused the pile up a few years before was evident. It was a recurring joke that when the firemen (who'd had to cut her out of her car) were all set to cut away her fur coat as well, Carla in a semi-conscious state had suddenly come to. *"Don't you dare!"* she'd squealed.

"No,"

"Exactly."

"I meant 'no' to quarantine, self-isolation whatever the hell you want to call it."

At last, she had his attention. Seb set down his phone and accelerated, running his hand over the top of his head, through the length of his hair. It was something he did when he was tired. Somehow it kept him awake.

"Wait, you're saying, you *won't?*"

"That's precisely what I'm saying."

And then she had pulled her large LV cashmere scarf close around her disguising her feeling of triumph. It was a small victory - payback for other wrongs, but there was no denying how his frown delighted her, how his bewilderment was a bonus. She felt an urge to giggle. He didn't.

"Seb," she said placidly because the more upset he became, the more detached she felt. "*Of course*, I care what happens to you but let's be realistic. You aren't at risk - you just aren't in that category. We've been nowhere *near* any infection."

"Except for that woman on the plane."

Carla made a clicking sound. "She had a *cold*."

"A dry cough."

"It was chesty."

"Those *are* the symptoms of this virus."

"Oh, for goodness' sake!" snapped Carla "You don't know that. Look," she placed a hand on his thigh, which he ignored. "*Calma cariño, sé calma.*"

He was anything but. "*You* be calm."

"I am."

"I can't believe you wouldn't do this. For me."

Carla rolled down the window just for a quick breath of country air. It was clean and crisp after the saprotrophic sweetness of Cartagena. She would let him talk although she had to concede her part in this. She *could* diffuse things by agreeing to his request, but then he would accuse her of lying when she reneged. She knew she was in store for a lecture. No doubt he would pull in the past, in addition to a list of grievances which could go on for a while as he reminded himself of her shortcomings. Nor would it end there. It was a conversation that could extend into the early hours of the morning. He might even wake her up to remind her, to itemise the points (just in case she'd forgotten) so that come morning, they could begin all over again.

In the beginning, Carla had indulged him although she hadn't thought of it as an indulgence - she would have called it honesty. But she quickly learned it was neither. There was something in him, some twist that could suddenly alter the lovely closeness between them. She was no better now though. It wasn't point scoring as such, and it was destructive, chipping away at what they'd once had. Would it make a difference now she wondered if he'd been different then? Would her answer be different if *that* hadn't happened? Would she move her hand from his thigh to pat his arm, tell him once again to keep his eyes on the road *mi amor,* while promising to follow him wherever he was going? To self-isolation and beyond? *I'll do whatever it takes to preserve your life,* she *should* be saying, *because you are my life.*

"This is ridiculous."

Suddenly Carla's mood took a dive, the elation at being home evaporating just as quickly as the cold Hampshire air blasting through the car. In contrast, flashes of colour and the heat that was Cartagena sprang before her eyes. Had it really been so blisteringly hot only forty-eight hours earlier? It was no ordinary heat either, but the kind that quite literally sucked the life out of you, plugged your eardrums with dust and filled your nostrils with the scent of overripe mango. It was a thirst-inducing heat, alleviated only by coconut sellers plunging machetes through the hard fruit's carcass to release fragrant, refreshing liquid. Half comatose, they had wandered jewel-coloured streets marvelling at the filigree balconies and the salamander door handles of its Colonial buildings. No wonder Gárcia Márquez had written about magic realism - Carla had felt it there in spades.

"You aren't ill. There's nothing to worry about."

Seb's shoulders hunched as he shifted in his seat. "You don't know that."

Carla muttered something indistinct.

"What did you say?" His fleshy lips pursed, the very lips she had once found so unbelievably sexy. In fact, she had once found everything about him so drop-dead sexy that she'd have happily isolated with him from here to eternity.

"No," she replied, raising her voice just a little. "You're right; I don't know that."

They passed Winchester Service Station. Polyphemus's aria in Act II, 'O ruddier than the cherry' was playing. She knew it at once. They had been to see *Acis and Galatea* at the Covent Garden when they'd first started dating - well if you could call their clandestine affair 'dating'. Anyway, when things had been so much more complicated and yet so very simple. Maybe he also remembered, because he held out his hand in a conciliatory gesture. She hesitated (he didn't notice) before responding. Warmth pulsated from his large steady hand as he raised hers to his lips. Just as quickly the slow-burning spark that threatened to become something more, was extinguished, the sudden rebellion in her, quashed. Until next time. But that was the problem, they never really resolved the issues that flared up between them. With a sinking feeling, a part of her knew that it would always be like this. The other questioned whether she would ever have the strength to resist him, bound up as they were in each other's secrets. There was confusion, too much raw passion, too much hurt. And for a moment if she allowed it, she could be transported, she could remember how it was.

2

It took Carla less than half an hour to unpack. She'd returned with laundered clothes, carefully distributed among her Paravel packing cases - all embroidered with her initials 'CC' - Carla Cave. Carla wasn't quite used to owning such a short name. She'd been born with three, gone down to two when she married Angus and now had only one. "*Cheer up!*" said Seb when she'd commented (not entirely flippantly on the pitifully few letters). "*Think of it as a distortion of the Chanel logo.*" Carla traced the embroidery with the tip of a manicured fingernail. Initials or no, they travelled so frequently that the packing cases saved on time. Once home, it was merely a question of transferring the cases to her 'summer' bag to be stored away until their next hot holiday. Carla was meticulous. She also had a 'skiing' bag ready for the winter season. But this attention to packing wasn't only because she was passionate about her clothes, it was because space up until now had been a premium and she'd had to be well organized.

Pouring the few travel-size toiletries into the respective containers in her bathroom, Carla enjoyed being able to move around without bumping into the edge of the bath or banging her head on the medicine cabinet. They'd moved to this new house a mere few weeks before going to Colombia. The holiday had been booked long before they'd even thought about moving again. They'd already moved once from a large manor and had been renting for a while. But their place was tiny. This new house had a whole floor in the attic that would be perfect for Alfie, so that when it came up, Carla had leapt at the chance to view it.

But on the given morning she'd had misgivings. Apart from the tiny rooms and absence of cupboards, the most significant advantage to their current house, was privacy. Situated directly in front of the city walls, it was quieter than her place in the country had been. Living on a narrow street, hemmed in on both sides by former workmen's cottages would be another matter altogether. *"Read my lips,"* she had mouthed as Seb dragged her up Canon Street. *"I'm never living here. Never."* *"Just take a look, that's all you have to do - as a baseline from which to move,"* he'd replied calmly. *"We've nothing to lose."* In the rain, hugging her reversible mink parka she'd smiled grimly at the estate agent who stood waiting for them, her bicycle propped under the window of the house. *"Never!"* she hissed again for good measure behind the woman's back as she struggled with the massive locks. Seb made a pushing movement with his hands by which he meant she should bottle it. Or keep her voice down.

All three of them had stumbled headlong into the hall as the door suddenly gave way, and Carla was wedged against the agent's soft bosom. Her cry had become elongated - shock anticipating the inevitable tumble (Seb's iron-like grip broke her fall) rising to a crescendo of delight. From the outside, the house appeared no different from any of the other small cottages along the street. Inside, it couldn't have been more different. A wide limestone corridor ran the entire length of the house to the flint and brick-walled garden beyond. The effect was one of light, and glass and stone and modernity. But most of all of space.

"We'll take it."

Seb didn't even blink. He knew her so well (one of the annoying things about him) - the seductive part - the part that kept Carla cemented to him.

"You heard her," he said to Vicky, the estate agent. "If my wife decides something ..."

Vicky smiled, eyes happily alert. This was an easy sale. She'd taken it on knowing that it would be. A house like this, on a road like this, in a town like this ...

But Carla wasn't listening. She had raced through the house, taking the stairs two at a time as if the place was already theirs, as it was already in her mind. Already she was sizing up the rooms wondering where their baby grand piano would go - *if* it would go at all - wondering at the funny interior room that would have to be a dining room, not minding too much either way and sold of course on the attic rooms for Alfie and the enormous bathroom with the roll-top tub that she wouldn't share with anyone, that would be hers alone. Not even the grey day and fine drizzle could dampen her excitement, nor extinguish the smoke rings of hope floating through her mind. If she could soothe the shards of pain and her instinct, she could go on. In a house like this, she knew she could, a bit longer.

Her eldest daughter had different ideas. Sophie was an accountant working in Portsmouth, whose mind was a steel trap especially honed for audits with her mother. Carla hadn't had the courage to speak to her directly, but she was so elated she wanted to share the excitement with someone. From the top floor - the wood-panelled room with its floor-to-ceiling bookcases and exposed beams and darling little twin-bedded alcove that would be Alfie's - she texted her daughter.

We're moving. Ping. Carla had pressed 'send' before including an 'x' which she now hastily added. But in between sending the second, she glanced over the rooftops to the shimmering view of the Cathedral, its Lancet windows visible above vertical mullions. Stick thin figures had emerged to walk the length of the nave roof.

All of you?

The meaning was clear.

And there it was, shot down in flames - the glorious diaphanous balloon of hope. A hope that the past might be forgotten - that the past might be *forgiven* - was exposed again, splattered and bleeding all over her face. She had taken a deep breath as though Sophie were actually with her, before replying:*Yes, all of us.*

Now, Carla had a quick shower holding the telephone handle ever so carefully so as not to chip the bath. These roll tops were beautiful but impractical too - she virtually held her breath every time she used it. She didn't dare risk a bath but not for fear of damaging the enamel. She was confident that if she lay down anywhere, even in a tub, fatigue would overcome her. Better to be refreshed and keep going. Alfie would be home later, and she wanted to be alert for him. She patted herself dry in front of the full-length mirror. Her body was still trim, and it was certainly smooth and tanned, but when had her neck become so, well, frankly *scrawny*? She peered closely. Was that her actual jawline? Were those *jowls*? How was that possible when her face was *thin*? When had she gotten older? She'd not noticed. Maybe it was because their old house hadn't had any long mirrors, so that she'd only ever seen her body in sections - face or feet or midriff but never all together. She'd been too busy moving recently and travelling before, to notice the alterations. She looked away. She was tired. It wasn't the moment to think too introspectively - not the time for vanity. Or at least no more than usual.

She went into her dressing room and pulled out a pair of leather leggings and a cashmere sweater. Leaving her hair wet, she went downstairs barefoot, taking pleasure in the underfloor heating - her toes splayed, heat penetrating each metatarsal. When she'd told a friend about it, the friend had seemed mystified. Why would anyone want underfloor heating? Well, she could answer that now. It was utterly delicious.

Seb was at the stove splashing milk into a saucepan. With his back to her, in his jeans and white shirt, he looked no different from when they'd first met.

"They've declared a state of emergency in Spain," he announced grimly. He liked to give her news about the country of her birth, no matter how bleak. He was folding oats into boiling milk with a wooden spoon.

Carla was almost salivating; she was so hungry. She fished out the new reed placemats from the shopping bag he'd brought in from the car and which she'd bought from a chi-chi boutique near Sir Francis Drake's house in Cartagena. She'd been surprised that the Colombians should want to acknowledge the infamous pirate who had burned and looted their beautiful city before been driven off by another 'beeruus' - an infection that had killed hundreds of his crew. Now, refusing to think about disease of any kind, Carla consoled herself with the fact that the chartreuse colour looked beautiful on the mango wood table delivered just before they left for their holiday. Her Spode china looked especially pretty against it. A pot of tea was waiting, milk in the jug, honey and a banana by her setting. Just as she liked it. Seb was good at the small details that made for harmony. If she thought only about those …

"Why?"

"*Why?*"

"Yes, why?" Carla slid onto her chair, tweaked the layout, straightening the cutlery. "It's ridiculous. Typical Spaniards to overreact. *Everyone -*" She said to Seb's back although he was too absorbed by his cooking to notice, "is overreacting."

"I don't think so," Seb said quietly. He took the pot off the fire and covered the mixture allowing it to thicken. He turned to face her. "Italy is in total lockdown. There's no travel, no restaurants, no hotels, no theatre. Nothing at all. Everything was calm in your country until a couple of days ago. When cases tripled in twenty-four hours."

"Oh," said Carla although she felt like saying 'oops' and it's not really *my* country any more, but they'd already had a few near misses in terms of arguments - no point in fanning the flames on another. It was true that she hadn't kept up to speed with news while they were away. Exhausted by the move, tormented yet again by what had been (well that was always by degrees - there wasn't a day that went by that she didn't think about it) and responsible for a future she had somehow engineered, she'd made the conscious decision to avoid all newsfeed choosing instead to read about the life of Simon Bolivar. There was enough Spanish in her, however, to make it impossible for her to accept Bolivar as a 'liberator.'

"The Prussian army at the gates of Madrid," she said more to herself. Except during that campaign Spain had been freed, not imprisoned. Carla had read history at university and still thought of most events in terms of the nineteenth century.

"What?"

"I mean it must feel like it."

Seb turned back to his porridge, giving it a final stir before bringing the pot to the table. He spooned it into their bowls. Piping hot, steam rose in graceful, thin spirals.

"I don't know about that, but I do know that it must be terrifying. I don't think we fully appreciate what's being going on while we were away."

"I know," she conceded. Head bowed, she sliced banana into her bowl, then poured honey onto the mixture.

"No," said Seb thoughtfully, "No, we don't. Not at all."

Carla took a mouthful of the delicious porridge, then poured piping hot tea into her mug. Somehow, tea abroad never tasted the same - she supposed it was on account of the water. She cupped the mug in her hands, allowing it to cool. Her eyes flicked around her new kitchen. It was lovely: pale wood and darker Corian worktops. Natural light not only came through a skylight and French windows but bounced off the large mirrors she'd placed opposite. She struggled with the concept of 'pandemic' or 'contagion.' In China, perhaps but here?

Carla let Seb talk on, rattle off statistics that meant little to her, field work calls and text his only brother who lived in America. Unlike Carla, Seb had not been married before. She had twins from her marriage to Angus, but Alfie was hers and Seb's. She felt a stab of excitement at the thought of seeing their twelve-year old son. She would tidy up and change again before collecting him from the school that was yards from the house. She looked forward to seeing her friends, whom she'd not seen since they moved. She'd catch someone and ask them back for an early supper. The thought cheered her.

Seb threw down his phone and poured himself a final cup of coffee. The liquid splashed in the mug and she winced as it seeped into the all-too-recently sealed table. She jumped up to grab a cloth.

"Dom says I'm vulnerable. I'm going to order an oxygen cylinder." He picked up his phone again and began googling furiously. "And a mask. Might as well have that too. Christ and a *valve*. Forgot about that!"

Carla's own phone pinged. She pushed her chair from the table, taking her bowl to the sink with one hand.

"*Sophie!*"

She tried to temper the delight she felt at hearing her daughter's voice. Sophie seldom called spontaneously, and if she did, it was generally in response to a call of Carla's.

"Darling! "*Most precious angel - my firstborn (by a minute) - my joy. My eternal guilt.* She wanted to say but didn't. The silence was resounding, fathomless. Something was wrong, but Carla knew she shouldn't ask outright, that she was expected to decipher an unspoken code.

But when she could wait no longer, knew that it was safe to ask, said, "Are you all right?"

Sophie's voice sounded muffled but friendly. "No, I'm not. I've never felt so ill."

It took Carla a moment to digest the words, they were said so cheerfully.

"Oh, sweetheart - it's not -" a hand of dread gripped her throat. So much so, that Seb sensing her fear, looked up, pausing his own texting. She shook her head and turned away from him. Was it this new virus? Was she being punished for not taking it seriously enough? What exactly had Seb said? She'd zoned out when she was reassured that it didn't seem to affect the young. So far. But had he actually said 'so far' or was that what she'd thought at the time? Sophie was convulsed by such a spasm of coughing, Carla had to hold the phone away from her ear.

"That sounds terrible." More coughing. "Look, don't try and talk just now. Text me when you've caught your breath, and I'll come over."

Sophie gave a final wheeze and rang off. But the text came through instantaneously - *when you're ill you only want your mum - shit! you must think I'm dying! That* sounded more like her daughter. *Not sure about the language girl!* Still, Carla couldn't remember a time when Sophie had asked for her.

Carla texted back: *OK let me change and I'll be over*

Seb looked up. This time, all warmth was removed from his expression.

"You're not thinking of seeing Sophie, are you?"

Carla paused on her way out of the kitchen. A tightening of stomach nerves - the desire to respond defensively.

"She's ill."

"Yeah, and so are a zillion others! That's kind of the point. Look, there are over a thousand confirmed cases in this country and some twenty people have died. I'm high risk," he sighed. "I thought we'd been through this."

Twenty didn't seem that much to her - nor the number of cases. Didn't more people die of the flu every year?

"We don't *know* that Sophie has the 'beeruus' - sorry virus. It's probably just a cold."

"She *always* has a cold."

"Exactly. Look," said Carla on a different tact. "I'll only *see* her. I won't touch her."

He looked at her. "And what about Alfie? We're talking about an acute respiratory virus. You do know what that means? For Alfie? Or had you forgotten?"

Carla blinked. *Stay calm.* She had not forgotten about Alfie. If her daughter had a persistent cough, Alfie had persistent bronchitis. They'd seen countless specialists who all said the same thing. His was a passing cold or allergy-related. He'd grow out of it.

"Everyone has said he'll grow out of it," she said evenly. "I'm not worried about Alfie."

Carla's mobile pinged again. All school matches for Saturday were cancelled. Damn. Another thing to which she was looking forward. Carla relayed the news.

"So, it's beginning," said Seb. "We're catching up."

"What do you mean?"

"With France and Italy? The London marathon's been cancelled, the Six Nations versus Scotland, all Premier League matches and local elections. Wake up, Carla! What do you think's been happening?"

Carla said nothing. Doing his best to stall her, Seb launched into a quick list of all the disasters occurring abroad. And here. Everyone over the age of seventy was being told to self-isolate.

"Sophie never asks for anything," she said weakly. She felt a sudden rush of fatigue - the imaginary sensation of a plane hitting turbulence.

Her phone pinged.

Just spoke to my GP and he's trying to sort out a CV test so if you want to stay away totally understand - am just on hold to 111

CV? Goodness thought Carla, what on earth was a CV test? Was it something to do with cystic fibrosis? She shrank from Seb's questioning look.

"Sophie's talking to her GP," she said brightly. "No urgency. At least I don't think so."

She texted Sophie.

I will never stay away… but it may be later

Sophie's response was relaxed, friendly. *Fine no worries*

A few moments later, another came through:

Let me know when you're 30 minutes away as I'm out and about doing a few bits

"Yes?"

She could tell Seb was counting the number of pings. She switched her phone to silent.

Carla re-read Sophie's text. If Sophie was 'out and about doing a few bits' then she couldn't be that unwell, could she?

"Yeah, she's fine."

"It's already 2 p.m.," said Seb. "Alfie will be home soon."

"I know and I realise that there's no time to go to Portsmouth. Looks like Sophie's a bit better, so panic over. You can relax."

Great, Carla texted taking a deep breath, *but might be tomorrow now. Running late to collect Alfie*

Phone in hand, she sprinted upstairs to grab a cardigan and change her shoes. *Do you need anything?* She added, hoping Sophie would skip past the first bit, concentrate on her offer. *Anything at all.*

No reply. Carla was able to dig out a pair of peach, soft-as-butter Tods and drape a tan cashmere sweater around her shoulders before Sophie texted back:

I'll be home by 3.30

It was another couple of hours, just as Carla was settling down to answer emails and check to see if she was needed in court - she did ad hoc (very ad hoc - in fact even less than ad hoc - almost ad nothing) translation for the law courts - that Sophie again texted:

What time were you planning on getting here?

Er … Carla did a panic scroll upwards. She wasn't … at least not today, not any more. Had she missed something? Hadn't she said *maybe* tomorrow? Carla scrutinised every word. Oh dear, the 'can I get you anything?' could have implied that she'd be over soon. As in today. And then to her relief, Sophie texted:

Don't worry if you can't

Carla sent twenty emojis: kisses and hearts and lips and balloons and a cake. Earlier she could have driven over and been back in time for Alfie, but not now, now she was also exhausted.

I'll come over the weekend - promise

Phew! Carla was off the hook. She would go and see Sophie some time in the next few days when she'd caught up on some sleep. What a relief though not to have to get into a car now and go anywhere! Jetlag was definitely kicking in. Snuggling back into her chair and kicking off her shoes, Carla continued checking her calendar. She looked at her bookings for the month. Not many. Interpreting was something she still enjoyed, but demand (if only there were!) for her services was dwindling. Everyone had a few words of Spanish these days. Or rather, it was the other way around - most Spaniards had enough English to make themselves understood.

Actually, it was Seb who'd encouraged Carla to go back to work when they'd first met. He wanted her to be sufficiently occupied so that he could play polo uninterrupted. What he'd not appreciated was that she might actually have to *go* to work. He'd never understood that she couldn't just drop everything when he wanted to spend a weekend playing in Deauville or fly to Marrakesh for a party. He'd almost been in contempt of court once when he'd thought it romantic (and hilarious) to burst in on a three-day trial and pull her out of the gallery. And all because he wanted to cadge a lift in his pro's Lear. As patron, he'd been offered a game in Sotogrande with one of the Hermès family and if there was one thing Seb could never resist, it was a good name being part of his team.

To begin with, she'd taken it all very seriously and stayed

behind and been miserable.

"*Do you trust him to go on his own?*" Friends had said.

"*Do you trust me to go on my own?*" Seb had said.

"*But it's you who wants me to work in the first place!*" she'd wailed.

"*You should want it for yourself.*" He'd implied that he thought less of her for being so conflicted.

"*I do.*"

"*Well, then.*"

"*Well, then.*"

Some of their biggest rows had concerned her working. And then she'd had Alfie, and the rows were no longer about her work. But it wasn't all Seb's fault. Her heart wasn't in it anymore, not like it used to be. Her heart, if she was honest, wasn't in much these days. Except for Alfie.

Her phone pinged. It was the Spanish boy's father. He'd arrived that morning from Madrid to collect his son, but she wasn't entirely off the hook.

I can't find masks or hand disinfectant or loo paper anywhere in London, can you help?

3

A couple of hours later, when the doorbell rang, Carla greeted her son with mixed feelings. She was thrilled to see him, of course. They'd only spoken a handful of times while they'd been away as their attempts to reach him had been frustrated by the time difference. However, she was disappointed he'd not waited for her in the schoolyard. Carla had been looking forward to seeing some of the other mothers and chatting with her friends. There might also have been the opportunity to check on Alfie's progress with his teachers.

"Darling!" she exclaimed guiltily aware that her pleasure was tinged with dismay. As usual, Alfie looked as if he'd slept in his clothes. She clicked her tongue at undone shoelaces and elbow patches that appeared to have slipped along the forearm of his tweed jacket. The jacket didn't even look as if it belonged to him. She wondered why mothers spent so many frantic hours sewing name tapes onto clothes. A far more sensible approach would be to contribute the school uniform to a communal bin where boys could help themselves. Ah, yes, that's *precisely* what her son did. With his feet pointing in first position, he looked like Charlie Chaplin. Her eyes travelled downwards. "Good heavens! Where are your socks?"

Alfie brushed the hair out of his eyes. "Hush grand bébé," he said. "It's fine. We've just had games It's fine."

"I know, and you're going to tell me you didn't have time to change?"

"The games socks are really itchy."

"So you don't wear them." It wasn't a question. She opened the door wide. "I give up."

As he scraped past, he did a quick about-turn, rugby tackling her. She staggered backwards. He'd become much stronger recently. Her lips lingered on his head. His hair smelled dirty. She wondered when he'd last changed his shirt, let alone had a shower. Didn't anyone check the boys' hygiene? She was about to shut the door when she noticed that Alfie had used his skateboard to transfer a hessian sack full of school books.

"What's this?" she said. "I don't understand. You don't break up until *next* Friday."

Alfie shrugged his shoulders. Sudden tears spilled over mud-stained cheeks, and now that she looked at him closely, the spidery veins under his eyes were microscopic and mauve.

"Hey big guy," said Seb coming down the stairs. Alfie threw himself at his father. They had a very close relationship, closer than hers was with him, she thought with a pang. Seb enveloped Alfie in a bear hug lifting him clear off the ground.

"We were told to bring everything home," said Alfie his voice cracking.

"That's fine," said Seb.

"For an *exeat*?" Carla felt panic rise in her throat.

"For the rest of the term," said Seb.

There was a stunned silence. That is Carla was stunned, Seb couldn't help grinning at the expression on her face.

"What do you mean?"

"Just had an email," said Seb. "They're sending the boarders home early."

Alfie had begun lugging his books across the threshold, and they scattered like a game of dominoes onto the flagstone floor - some upright, some falling open. He kicked off his shoes by her new Gustavian desk. She winced as they hit its slender legs. Carla held up her hand, blocking any further progress down the hall. They now had a hall down which they could all fit abreast. In their previous postage stamp townhouse, they'd had to pass each other sideways.

"But this isn't all your gear?" The thought occurred to Carla that if she hurried, she could still go back to the school and her friends would still be there.

"Yeah, it is." During their brief embrace, Alfie had managed to winkle Seb's phone out of his pocket and was texting furiously.

"No, it isn't."

Again, Seb made that pushing gesture he did when he wanted Carla to calm down or lower her voice. Preferably both.

"He says that's all he has."

Carla glared at him.

"He's come home with *books*," she explained patiently," but I don't see a pencil case, fountain pen (the expensive ink pen with the rubber bear top they'd bought in Switzerland), home clothes of any description, shoes, not to mention *socks*. We're going back. If he - *you're,*" she faced her son, "coming home, then you need your stuff. Come on we'll nip back together."

"No."

"*Yes!*" She bent down to hand him his shoes. "Let's go."

"I'll go," said Seb.

"No, it's fine. I'll go." Nothing was going to stop her now. Already she anticipated the enthusiastic responses at her appearance - especially her lovely new Tods. She wanted to see her girlfriends. The mothers of the boys in Alfie's class were always so complimentary, so sweet. She hadn't realised until that moment how much she enjoyed seeing them. At this moment Carla *needed* to see them as though they would somehow make her feel validated. By being complimented, she existed. "I'll go," she repeated.

Sulkily, Alfie shovelled his feet into his shoes without undoing the laces, flattening the backs.

"Oh, my goodness," she said, annoyed. "No wonder they don't last!"

"Whatever." Alfie made a face, thrusting his fists into his pockets.

Carla began marching down Canon Street. This wasn't at all how their homecoming was supposed to be.

"Come on!" she barked. And when Alfie hadn't quickened his pace, she quickened hers. "I'll see you in the yard then."

She knew he'd mouthed another 'whatever,' but she let it go. She'd see her friends first, deal with him later although she had to remember that they'd been away, and this was Alfie's way of getting back at her. The twins had been the same when she'd come home after being absent for any length of time. And she knew she was being just a tad unreasonable. She had trouble processing so much new, fast-changing information. But Alfie did, in fact, hurry.

The air was fragrant with lilac and the magnolia at the corner of College Street was in full bloom, its pink waxy flowers vibrant against the cloudless sky. Peeping above brick and flint, a cherry's delicate white petals were strewn across the narrow patch of grass by the central arch. Carla waited for her son in front of Jane Austen's house. Alfie walked towards her along the low wall as he used to when he was little. He jumped down barrelling into her. His face was soft against her neck, and she felt his warm, boyish form.

"Sweetheart, I don't mean to be grumpy. I'm sorry. Let's get the rest of your stuff and go home." She squeezed his arm while he punched in the code on the door's keypad. They continued in single file down the narrow passage that led into the schoolyard. The creaky door opened. But the ta-da! moment she'd anticipated as they emerged onto the yard with friends rushing towards them, didn't happen. Instead, her smile fading, she stopped short, confused. The 'yard', usually buzzing with activity, with boys playing cricket at one end, shooting balls into a basket at the other; with choristers lining up in their black cloaks ready to be escorted to Evensong and snacking on Bourbon biscuits, was virtually empty.

Typically, mothers clustered in groups according, but not

limited to, the ages of their children. Teachers came and went in various combination of sports clothes. Parents with pets on a leash hovered on the other side of the yard behind the main gates. And behind those gates, ancient and magnificent was the Cathedral, casting a protective presence with regular peels of reassurance. Now, more than ever, it was a timely reminder of what had been before and what would endure.

Only it wasn't like that at all. There was an unearthly silence, not a boy or an adult in sight. Certainly, no parents and suddenly her own toned, bronzed skin seemed a luxury that was completely irrelevant at this time. She fingered the expensive silk at her throat, the familiar comfort of two-ply cashmere at her hip. Alfie scuffed his worn shoe even further, but for once Carla let it go. To her question of "Where is everybody?" He merely shrugged and then from a diagonal passageway that led to the 'Octagon', the sports master - a large former rugby player and someone she'd known for fifteen years - someone who was perennially tranquil and good-humoured, hurried not towards her, but to a door behind. Alfie recoiled while her own smile of greeting froze.

"The rest of his clothes? His ..."

Mr. Ganzi's eyes narrowed - without the slightest warmth or glint of amusement with which he usually greeted her. If she didn't know him better, from that one look, she might have thought he actively disliked her. Maybe he did - at any rate, she might as well have been invisible, and he wasn't stopping to chat.

"He was told to clear out his Toy." Mr. Ganzi used the slang Winchester boys call their individual study cubicle. "He should have done it by now."

"Yes, well, you know - Alfie - never -" her voice faded. It was clear that Mr. Ganzi couldn't have cared less about Alfie. He seemed to have much more pressing matters on his mind. And she hadn't brought any bags with which to clear out a desk, let alone a whole study.

"It's fine, Mum," muttered Alfie embarrassed now. "It's fine. We can go. I've got everything I need."

"Well, you clearly don't," said Carla. "What about the Chilly water bottle Sophie gave you and the book your godfather sent you for Christmas? Wink wink." Xavier, Alfie's godfather, had sent Alfie a 'book'. The pages had been cut out to create a hole and then filled with sweets. He'd used the very same book to hide cigarettes when he'd been at school. *'Not of course suggesting you do that!'* he'd scrawled on a card. Typical Xavier. Tears spurted in his eyes. "It's too late, anyway," he said wiping his cheeks roughly. "They've locked the Toys. I'll have to wait till next term."

Carla's temple had begun to throb, but her son's sudden upset took her aback. She was clearly missing something and if she was finding the fast pace with which everything seemed to be moving strange and bewildering, how much more so must Alfie be feeling it? After all, there was no precedent for this - whatever 'this' was. She was about to thank Mr. Ganzi, but he had already disappeared into one of the music rooms swallowed up by the shadows and shapes of abandoned instruments. She clasped Alfie to her. "I'm sorry, I'm sorry," she said full of remorse. "Let's go home. We can get your things some other time. It's lucky that we live so close, isn't it? Imagine if it had been the old house?"

Mention of the 'old house' was a mistake. After the car crash, she and Seb had been involved in a few years before, they'd come to the difficult decision to sell their lovely old manor house in the middle of the countryside. Tiredness had definitely played a part in the accident when they realised so much driving was taking its toll. Never having lived in a city before, Carla loved the novelty of being able to walk to the shops, to Alfie's school, to meet friends for a coffee. Both she and Seb enjoyed the rich cultural life the city had to offer in the form of concerts, theatre and film. No, in the end, it had been a blessing. Alfie hadn't quite seen it that way and had cried most nights for months after they moved. As he got older, however, he too could see the advantages: friends who lived within walking distance, no commute and he could sleep in until twenty minutes before classes began, if he really wanted. Even when he began boarding, he would pop in most days just to say hello, check his messages (he didn't have his own phone) or just escape the claustrophobia of school life even if only for a short time.

When Alfie didn't respond, she added quickly. "How about a Hershey's bar from the KPO?" Carla still referred to the local shop - Kingsgate Post Office (no longer a post office) by its acronym.

"Can we just go home?"

Walking with her arm still draped around him, she gave him another squeeze.

"'Course we can," she said, but she felt chastened. She had never known her son turn down an offer of sweets before.

4

"It's no longer 'partial'," said Seb cheerfully at breakfast the next morning. "We're officially on complete lockdown." Carla had slept solidly for nine hours exhausted less by their long journey from Cartagena, than by the shock of Alfie's school term ending ten days early. She padded downstairs in her robe, taking fresh delight in the airiness of their new house, the lovely warm tiles underfoot, the reflections of light on so much glass. To Carla's mind, the first days in a new home were always invigorating. She loved the sense of hope a new place brought, the potential for a life unlived. Her hand traced the lovely oak bannister.

She had so many plans - a blank space either side of the antique French mirror reminded her that she had pictures on order from the States. They would need framing - *framing*. She frowned, she *wished* now that she'd bought those Robert Adam prints that she had viewed at auction just before they'd left for South America and *not* listened to Seb who'd restrained her from bidding any higher. *They* wouldn't have needed framing. And now that her mind had tacked to retail regret, she also wished Seb hadn't talked her out of buying those adorable tan leather sandals she'd thought were priced at $375 - *American* - not Colombian; a song as opposed to a small fortune.

But she had come home with her reed placemats and by hers, was a paper heart with the words, 'Be My Quarantine' scrawled across it. She blinked uncomprehending, taking time to focus without her contact lenses. Of course! She'd forgotten all about the 'beeruus.' The imprint of her white slab of a pillow, cool, oblivion-inducing still visible on her cheek.

"Cute," she muttered, having no intention of being quarantined, or isolated or spending a minute longer inside than she had to. They weren't going to start all that nonsense, again were they? Besides, there were operas in the diary with dinner in the Hamlin Hall beforehand, and more importantly Tom, her older son's graduation from Oxford - she still hadn't decided what she was going to wear to that - and the usual round of end of term, summer parties. This being Alfie's final year at prep school, there'd be even more than usual with extra cocktails and picnics. Maybe a silk jumpsuit to one and the Missoni to the other.

Seb shook his head as if reading her mind. He made coffee with the Colombian beans they'd bought in Cartagena, tightening his own dressing gown. Once the sight of his hairy chest would have made her stomach churn. It still did occasionally, but now it was a faint butterfly, the fragile flapping of wings rather than a whale-like lurch. His new preoccupation with this flu thing was becoming a turn-off.

"Ugh uh," he said. "Think I prefer Aldi coffee." He loaded a heaped teaspoon of sugar spilling more on to the table than into his mug. "That's better. Nope."

"Keep it for guests."

She brushed past him to open the French doors leading to the patio. She was curious to see what had appeared in the flower beds she'd not had time to examine before they left. She spotted herbs: sage and rosemary and a cutting garden. Along the middle path were primroses, forget-me-nots and pale green hellebores. She thought ruefully that she seemed destined to live with winter roses that were never very white. A rush of cold air made her close the door quickly. It might be spring, but the mornings were still raw.

"It's all off."

She turned back. "What the whole batch? Even if you add sugar?"

"Not the coffee. I mean everything."

"What everything?" she sat down at the table, moving the cut-out heart out of sight behind the teapot. "I know the Bensons have said it's up to us. They'll understand if we decide *not* to go, but they still want to, and I'm dying to see *Cavalleria Rusticana*. It's the one opera I've not seen. We *love* Covent Garden ..." her voice dwindled.

Seb seemed distracted but he continued laying the table. Every morning of their life together, he had got breakfast ready. In the old house, because it was so cold and getting out of bed equated to Scott of the Antarctic setting out on his final walk, he'd even brought her breakfast in bed.

"When did they say that? I mean, when did they reply?" he asked at length.

Carla shrugged. "Dunno - a few days ago - maybe an email when we were away? I ordered you a Caesar-" she took out her phone from her robe pocket, scrolling through her messages. "Then fillet."

She left the phone on the table reaching to sprinkle Grape Nuts onto her fruit and yoghurt. Seb always saw to it that they all had exactly what they liked to eat. There was a thoughtfulness that she loved and appreciated. But there was the other ...

Seb nodded sympathetically. "Things have moved on since

then. "All public gatherings have been cancelled," he took a sip of coffee and made a face. "Except funerals."

"Well we didn't have any of those in the diary."

"Let me double-check."

"Very funny." She looked behind him to the kitchen units. Already there were black scuff marks along the skirting board and dust under the thin space above the dishwasher. Nothing stayed new for very long. "But not opera?"

"Definitely opera. All gatherings of more than 500 people."

"Well that's ridiculous."

"Ridiculous or not, that's how it is. I've had a refund too from that talk we were going to at the English-Speaking Union. And Ascot. And the ENO and-"

"OK, OK." It was too early to digest so much depressing news. She took a mouthful of fruit, washed it down with tea. "Fine," she said, marvelling at her own fortitude. "We'll just have to have lots of dinner parties."

Seb pushed away his breakfast, getting up to put a couple of Weetabix in the bowl she just noticed he'd set for Alfie. Carla had forgotten their son was home. "Two hundred and eighty-one people have died from this virus," he explained patiently interpreting her blank expression as ignorance. "And if you understand *anything* about statistics and the increase exponentially-"

"Yes, yes," interrupted Carla impatiently. "But everyone who's died has been old and suffered underlying health issues. Surely the way to judge if this is a lethal disease is to look at the death rates and see if more people are dying than we'd expect them to at this time? Frankly, I don't see what the issue is. Don't more people die of normal flu?"

Seb considered her. "They do, but that's kind of the point. If cases increase exponentially as I've just said, then our healthcare system couldn't cope. This virus isn't *like* ordinary flu. It's not similar to anything we've seen. I think it's a MERS or SARS but worse." Carla vaguely remembered the diseases that in recent years had gripped other parts of the world but hadn't really affected them here.

"Point taken," said Carla sulkily. "But isn't everyone always whining about the older population and what to do with it? Well, problem solved."

There was an uncomfortable silence.

"You didn't say that."

"I was joking," she protested feebly. *Sort of...* She added milk to the invisible Alfie's cereal. He liked it soggy. It was funny the way she and Seb were pandering to their son as though he were sitting in front of them. But then he could appear at any moment, and they liked to show willing, especially on his first day home. "Pandemics have happened throughout history," she continued. "They're not the exception. Viruses have been around for at *least* three hundred million years - why shouldn't we have another one now? I don't understand what the fuss is about."

"So, do I have the day off?" said a sleepy Alfie appearing in the kitchen - tousled and grubby and not looking too pleased with the prospect.

"Well, not if your mother's a key worker- the school will remain open to the children of those."

Carla's heart skipped a beat.

"Oh, my God! That's me!" she said joyfully.

Seb burst out laughing. "Define key worker, darling."

Carla went over to Alfie, rubbed his hair, kissed his cheek, straightened his cutlery and pushed his chair closer to the table.

"I'm a Mum," she said happily. "I look after kids."

"Sorry - doesn't count. Plus, technically, there's only one child at home."

Alfie shook his head, mashing his cereal.

"So, do I, or don't I?"

"Yup, big guy," said his father happily. "And tomorrow and the next day."

And the next.

"But I've got cricket today."

"Yes, think that might be off. Tell you what though, we can go down to the nets."

"OK," said Alfie, only partially mollified. "Can I borrow your phone? To check my messages?"

Carla made a face, but Seb countered. "It's fine; the boy needs the distraction."

Carla pushed her chair from the table. "And so, do I. I'm going to walk to the High Street, do a bit of shopping. Can I get you anything?"

"More paracetamol. Just in case."

Carla raised her eyes. They already had a pile.
They *always* had a pile. Every time Seb shopped at Aldi, he bought packets, it was so much cheaper than the High Street equivalent. She dropped another kiss on her son's head - it smelled stale - of boy and sweat. She wondered when he'd last showered. Carla knew that a familiar trick of her son's was to dampen his head after games and then get dressed - his knees and arms still caked in mud would be disguised by his clothing. She would coax him later into having a proper wash, but now she couldn't wait to be out of the house.

"There's a super spreader -" she heard Seb tell Alfie as she fled the kitchen. "An engineer who travelled to Britain from Singapore via the Alps. What do you think of that?"

Carla was confident Alfie didn't think much beyond the fact that his cricket season was on hold. She dressed in record time, then slipped quietly out of the house heading towards the church of St. Swithun-upon-Kingsgate. Medieval and tiny, it had originally been built into the very fabric of the city walls and was approached by a flight of slippery wooden steps. No bigger than a large room, with an uneven floor and low ceilings, it still managed to convey a sense of spirituality. Thin rays of sunlight flickered through its diamond-shaped stained glass. Carla loved that this little, innocuous church was the inspiration for St. Cuthbert's in Anthony Trollope's *The Warden*. And that if she turned to face in the opposite direction, she would see 'the spires of St. Thomas' mentioned in *Tess of the D'Urbervilles*. She continued her walk under the central arch keeping the Elizabethan timber-framed house that once served as stables to the priory, on her right. Petals were scattered over the triangle of grass in front of it, like a delicate veil of Brussels lace.

Carla breathed a sigh of relief. This virus thing was clearly an exaggeration. Life was normal here. There were people on bicycles, a few children on scooters. She smiled at strangers as she hurried past the Cathedral to grab a coffee from Café Monde. While it was being made, she chatted cheerfully to its owner, be-moaning the state of the world; the fact that the U.K. was following a model of what *might* happen. Moving on to the high street, she observed customers hurrying in and out of shops jostling one another as though it were Christmas. Carla suppressed a giggle. Every second person seemed to be hugging a giant pack of loo paper. The Spanish side of her leapt at the chance to poke fun. *Her* priorities were different. She was after good quality soap (TK Maxx in the Brooks Shopping Centre always had a good supply) and fresh flowers.

But whatever her thoughts on the subject, it was impossible to ignore the tension in the air - a fear that was palpable. Carla could still feel the movement of the plane, which wasn't helping her growing sense of displacement. It seemed hard to believe that only a few nights before, she and Seb had been drinking champagne by the sea. Seb - the man she had once considered to be her soul mate. And he still was - when she was able to repress the memory of that other thing - the thing that lay so close to the surface always threatening to erupt when something wasn't quite right or then again when it was, to tarnish something lovely. That was the problem with traumatic events - you fought them, you acknowledged them, you survived them. Or so you thought and then over time, they returned more robust than before, more tenacious, the recovery period in between considerably shortened.

At the entrance of her local M&S, shop assistants were barricaded behind buckets of daffodils and stands of confectionery and newspapers. All manner of potted plants, some in full flower, some to be grown at home, evergreens and dwarf orchids, made it seem more of a nursery than a general food store. Carla chose her flowers - cream narcissus - holding the stems away from her as water dripped over her shoes. On the way out, shoppers were handed free bunches of flowers - a backlog from Mother's Day. Carla declined. "Give them to someone else." She gestured to an imaginary crowd, feeling bountiful.

Her phone pinged, and she transferred her shopping bag to one hand digging into the depths of black suede with the other.

"Yeah, Mum," said Tom.

"Hello darling," said Carla breathlessly beginning to walk back the way she had come, past shoppers weighed down with loo paper. She felt frivolous with her meagre supplies. At least some people appeared to have benefitted from the free flowers.

"You might want to go and see Sophie."

Sophie ... Carla ought to have texted her. If Carla had forgotten that Alfie was in the house that morning, she'd also forgotten that Sophie had said she was ill.

"I was going to! I mean, I still am - but later this afternoon."

Carla could hear Tom's measured pace over the ether.

"Um ... you may want to go now. She's really not well."

Carla shifted the phone to her other ear.

"Yes - I know, but she was out-"

"Ed's called an ambulance."

Tom mentioned Sophie's boyfriend.

A hand of dread stopped Carla in her tracks.

"What do you mean? She was out and about yesterday. She said she was busy with things. I didn't think-"

"Yeah, well she's worse now and having problems breathing."

If Ed had called an ambulance and Tom was calling *her*... She was through the passageway alongside the Cathedral.

"OK - I'm almost home - just have to grab the car, and I'll be on my way. I'll call you when I'm en route."

Carla quickened her pace, breaking into a run as she rounded the Cornflowers. Its inviting window showcased pretty spring tableware and Easter eggs. Normally, Carla would have stopped for a chat with its owner. She mouthed a greeting and although a brave smile was exchanged in return, it barely disguised the same worry, incredulity and disbelief Carla was beginning to see on the faces of everyone around her. She pushed open her front door, dropping her flowers and soaps on the hall table.

"Got to go!" called Carla. "Sophie's in hospital."

"Wash your hands!" yelled Seb in response from his study door.

"I will. I will -"

"Too late!" Seb came to the landing his lips vibrating with fury. When he was angry, it was the part of his anatomy that seemed to be affected first.

"I was just going to," she lied. "But-"

He stood quaking with anger - a completely different person from the one she'd left at the breakfast table.

"You don't get it! Can you imagine how many surfaces you've touched on the way home? Just coming into the house alone? Let's see; I'm assuming that you started with a shopping basket. So, you touched that. Then you chose an item. You set that down, picked up another. Someone else came along, passed nearby and before you know it you've spread your germs - or they have to you. Add a sneeze-"

"'Kay- 'kay, keep your hair on," she muttered.

"*What* did you say?" said Seb instinctively touching his long locks.

And there it was - that insidious belligerence for which they were both responsible. Seb's tone, her tone, his annoyance at her unwillingness to take this 'beeruus' seriously, hers with him because he did. Well, hers always with him for in retaliation for before ...

"I really do have to go," said Carla dividing the flowers and picking out a bunch to take to her daughter.

"Sophie's ill. Ed's called an ambulance so if I leave now, *pero ya*," she said in Spanish for emphasis which she only did when no other words would do. "I'll be there to meet it."

"Sorry to hear about Sophie." Seb turned back to his study. "But you can't go."

Carla felt a rush of fury at being dictated to, coupled with the need to leave as quickly as possible.

"What do you mean? *Of course*, I'm going! I could kick myself for not having gone when we first arrived. I should have gone straight there - I was just so tired …" *and just a little bit lazy.* She looked at Seb pleadingly. She wanted him to acknowledge her dilemma, to agree that it wouldn't have been right to drive when she'd not slept in three nights (albeit the last in the luxury of Business Class), to remove this immense, ever present sense of guilt. *Help me out here … let's change this dynamic once and for all …*

"No, you're not - you can't go."

Carla blinked, felt herself flush. "Sophie needs me. You've *always* said that children come first." And he had. When they first met, he'd said he understood about the twins, that he would always understand where children were concerned. But that was before they'd had Alfie.

"This is different."

She held his look. "I'm going."

He didn't even wait to consider. "Then don't come back."

Carla felt tears prick her eyes. "Don't be daft."

"I'm not. I mean what I say. If you see Sophie, then don't come back into this house and if Sophie has Covid-19-"

"*Covid?*"

Seb made an exasperated sound. "It's what the WHO is calling it. 'Co' and 'V' for Coronavirus and 'D' for disease -"

"'19' for the year - yeah got it. We talked about this. We don't *know* Sophie has the '*bir*' - sorry virus." She rooted in the drawers of the Gustavian desk looking for the car keys. They were a one-car household, only using theirs to attend the odd social gathering outside Winchester. If they went to London, the theatre or opera, they travelled by train. The days of private planes and helicopters to flit between engagements were long gone. Bingo! Her fingers settled on the orange mink key chain.

"There's a pretty good chance she does. You said so yourself. She has breathing difficulties."

Yes, but that was a few days ago. Carla assumed Sophie was better.

Her heart was now hammering so painfully she was amazed Seb couldn't hear it, couldn't *see* it chiselling its way out of her rib cage. She checked her handbag to make sure that she hadn't removed her contact lens case. That was really the only thing she needed along with a credit card and phone.

"Look," she said more patiently than she felt. "We don't - *can't* know anything. I'm going, and that's the end of it."

Then," said Seb just as patiently, "don't come back. Not for two weeks."

Carla glared at him. She ought to have stood up to him a long time ago. She should have gone to see Sophie when they arrived.

"Fine. If I have to self-isolate, so be it."

She gave the front door a furious slam and ran to the car which was parked in College Street just around the corner from the house. She scanned the street, not immediately seeing their hatchback BMW. She zapped the air.

It might be better not to go... texted Tom.

Don't understand?

She lifted her arm, once again aiming at nothing in particular. And then, just as she was about to give up, her car's rear lights flashed. Moments later, Carla had driven off, heading to the motorway. With her hands-free Bluetooth, she called up Tom's number speaking into the air, ignoring his previous message.

"Just realised I don't have Sophie's number," she said. Tom had finally answered on her fourth go. "I mean I know what street she lives on-" Carla rattled on nervously. And that was only because once, a few years back when she and Sophie had been having tea at the now-defunct Saint George Tea Rooms, they'd got chatting to a Spaniard who said he lived in Portsmouth. When Sophie had asked where exactly, and he'd told her, she'd been spontaneous in her reply. "That's where I live!" Ah-ha! Carla had thought at the time. Gotcha! But knowing the name of the road was of only partial help.

"Yeah, I don't either."

"Don't be ridiculous," said Carla tetchily. "You must do."

"Nope."

"Well, Daddy then. *Someone* must have it. You have Ed's number. I know you do, because he messaged you. Text him!"

How could they not know where a member of their family lived? Carla didn't want to contrast this to the close, loving relationship many of her friends enjoyed with their offspring. Mothers and daughters who doted on each other, who shopped together, travelled together. The dislocated voice told her to prepare to turn left.

There was a pause.

"Maybe you'd better leave it," said Tom. "I mean it might be better not to see Sophie. It's not being responsible. If she does have the virus. Shouldn't you be thinking of Alfie and Seb?"

"I'm thinking of *Sophie*."

"In that case, don't go."

Carla felt a prick of irritation; the sometime hurt and disappointment but always all-consuming love that accompanied negotiations with her children. "Hang on. You called *me* remember. Now for goodness' sake, give me the house number."

"I don't have it."

"This is ridiculous. We're going around in circles here. I just don't believe you."

"Oh, I hope you're not driving in circles," said Tom.

"Very funny."

"I don't have it!" he insisted, but she could hear the smile behind his words.

"Look, darling. If I have to self-isolate after seeing Sophie, I'll self-isolate. I'd rather that then face the next twenty years of Sophie saying I wasn't there for her." *Which she would anyway …*

"Fair enough."

The Satnav indicated that she had reached her destination.

"I'm here now," said Carla, shaky with jetlag, shaky at not having driven for a while but triumphant at having defied Seb. She was here for her baby, for Sophie. Carla would scoop her up and take her to a hotel where they could self-isolate. Carla's mind did a mental sweep of hotels she'd heard about recently. Ah yes! They might even stay in one of those adorable treehouses at Chewton Glen. Oh, joy! She'd forgotten all about those! What fun it would be! They could climb up together - just like they'd done when Sophie was small. Carla's gardener had built the twins a tree house when they were children, complete with a thatched roof and tiny twin-size furniture. Carla had loved receiving proper invitations to tea and then climbing up the wooden ladder to sit on diminutive chairs beside dolls and teddy bears. It wouldn't be so very different now: they could sleep, have lovely food, cocktails and swim. Carla would apologise again for her choices.

She turned into a street lined with pebble dash houses. "So, what's the number?"

"You're breaking up Mum-"

Like hell I am thought Carla. It was the same technique Tom's father used when he decided a conversation was over.

Carla suppressed a sigh. No matter. She was pretty certain that her daughter lived at 104. Yes, that was it. She pulled over in front of the house. It wasn't particularly attractive, but it wouldn't be Sophie's 'forever home'. Sophie was an independent young woman; an accountant pursuing a good career. She answered to no one. Carla felt a stab of envy. She combed her hair with her fingers, shaking it over her shoulders and tightened the belt on her shirt dress. She grabbed the flowers. There, she was ready; she could cope.

A smile in place she moved towards the house and stopped dead. Visible through the window, an elderly woman was being fed a bowl of soup. For a moment, Carla was distracted.

There was something incongruous about the woman. Swathed in a fluffy pink dressing gown that was far too big for her, she looked like a live doll. Carla was beginning to wonder about herself and whether or not she'd simply imagined the old woman because she'd been thinking about the twins and their toys. Then very real tears pricked her eyes. She'd been so confident that she would find Sophie. How stupid it was not to have her address! How humiliating! She rang Tom's number again, but it was engaged and then just when she was about to howl with frustration, an ambulance eased its way into the street, coming to a stop in front of her.

"You're not here for Sophie Douglas-Elwes, are you?" she said, thanking providence for her turn of good luck as two men alighted. Neither wore hazmat suits or masks.

"No name love," one of them said. "Just a street number."

"Well, I have a name and no number!" Carla was triumphant. "She's my daughter, but I'll wait out here."

The men nodded kindly. "We'll go in and check her over and let you know."

Carla leant against her car.

The men rang the bell of the house next door to the lady in the pink dressing gown, and Sophie's boyfriend Ed came to the door, whisking them inside. Carla tried to catch his eye, but he kept his head down - not an easy thing to do at 6ft 7. She watched their shadows disappear into the house, merge as they went up to the front bedroom and then expand against the pulled blinds.

At last, Ed emerged alone.

"Can I come in?" Carla waved the flowers helplessly. Of course, she couldn't go in, not if they were at all infectious.

"Uh, no." He wouldn't or couldn't look at her. "You can leave the flowers. On the doorstep. But I've come out to tell you that Sophie doesn't want to see you."

Carla took a few moments to process the information. Tears sliced her cheeks. "Doesn't want to see …?" she echoed, trying to make sense of his words. She glanced at the narcissus in her hand, their scent no longer fragrant and dropped them at his feet, taking a step back quickly. "What? Is this because I didn't come the other day?"

Ed shoved his hands in his pockets, broad shoulders hunched. "Don't know. Just passing on the message."

"I'm not going anywhere," said Carla digging in her heels, wedging her shoe in the gap between the pavement and car. "I'm staying right here."

Ed shrugged again, looking at his own feet. He didn't answer, but he might as well have said, "Suit yourself."

5

Carla remained outside, maintaining a suitable distance by sitting on the low brick wall of the house directly opposite. From there, she also had a better view of what was going on upstairs. She could see the silhouette of the ambulance men against the drawn blind. They appeared to be joking with Ed, which Carla found reassuring. They wouldn't joke so much would they, if the situation was really serious? Carla felt transfixed, compelled to stay put, yet uncertain, upset, exhausted and wracked with guilt. She really should have gone to see Sophie the very minute that first text came through: *'when you're ill you only want your Mum.'*

When had she last seen Sophie? Carla knew exactly. She could count the times they'd met up in recent years, each meeting carefully committed to memory, each get-together shorter, the intervals between them longer, than the last. But the most recent was also the most painful and still a little bit raw. It had taken place the week before she and Seb left for South America, shortly after they'd moved into Canon Street. Sophie had texted suggesting lunch and Carla had been beside herself with excitement. And a little surprised given their last communication.

Carla had dressed carefully to see her daughter. Sophie might poke fun at her designer clothes, but she knew that Sophie was secretly proud of the way her mum dressed. She wasn't going to disappoint. Carla had opted for leather trousers, Prada ankle boots and a pretty, on-trend cashmere sweater with a zip. The only suggestion of its expensive providence was the hint of mink lining at the cuff.

With a sense of elation, she'd sped towards Portsmouth and with an even greater feeling of pride had parked in the excruciatingly narrow car park of the accountancy firm where her daughter worked. She savoured the thrill of having been invited to lunch by her daughter. Just like other mothers and daughters. Ordinary. Normal. Close.

Bursting with pride Carla gave her daughter's name to the receptionist, noting that Sophie had dropped 'The Hon' prefix. She resisted the temptation of adding '*Yes, I'm her mother.*' But then Carla wasn't given the opportunity to say more even had she wanted to. Sophie wasn't exactly hiding, but she hovered by the entrance, propping the door open with her foot for a quick get-away. Carla had hoped Sophie might show her around her office, but Sophie seemed keen to get going. Carla's dip for a kiss was ignored with an "Only have an hour" as though an embrace would somehow eat into her lunch hour.

Carla suppressed a quick spike of hurt, let herself be warmed instead by how poised Sophie was, elegant in a purple Max Mara jacket and Jimmy Choo heels. Carla felt a surge of affection. Carla had given Sophie her entire outfit. From time to time, Carla collated sets of work clothes - beautifully tailored suits, a good winter coat that would see her through her training and beyond, an expensive handbag - all designed to elevate her daughter's look. Sophie, who was as disinterested in clothes as Carla was passionate, accepted them grudgingly as no better than cast-offs which they sometimes were. Most of the time though, Carla went shopping with her daughter in mind and cut out the clothes tags when she got home, knowing that Sophie wouldn't accept them if she thought they were brand new or too 'designer.' It was complicated but then so was their relationship.

"That's fine, darling," said Carla as they set off at breakneck speed across the neighbouring park towards the town centre. Her "I know you're busy," swallowed up by a sudden gust of wind, and the traffic from the congested roads either side.

"What do you fancy?"

Carla knew better than to say it didn't matter, what do *you* want to eat? Sophie liked clarity, honesty, didn't suffer fools or indecision.

"Er ... a salad? Something light."

"Let's go to Neptune."

"So..." began Carla looking up from a menu that as far as she could make out didn't feature a single salad, nothing light whatsoever and consisted of variations on 'jerk' this or that.

"*So?*"

Carla was taken aback by Sophie's tone - so harsh and uncompromising that Carla couldn't think of a single thing to say. Luckily at that moment, the waitress arrived to take their order. Or was she a he? Carla spent the next few minutes trying to decide while Sophie greeted the young person enthusiastically as 'Linton' although the badge on her uniform clearly said 'Linda.'

"You think they swopped?" said Carla when 'Linda' had gone. Carla wiped away some crumbs left by a previous occupant.

Sophie's expression was blank.

Carla made a vague half gesture to her chest. "The tag?"

Sophie pulled out her phone and began texting. For a

moment, Carla thought Sophie hadn't heard her but then she glanced up, still tapping.

"Why would you think that?"

"Oh, no reason. I -" said Carla weakly. *Just wanted to make conversation...*

"Linda identified as a woman although she was born a man. Now she's non-binary."

"I see," said Carla uncrossing her legs. The table was so low she kept banging her knees and she worried about scratching her leather trousers.

"That's ... fine."

"*Fine?*" Sophie's immaculately groomed eyebrows shot up to the ceiling.

"All right maybe fine wasn't the right word. I'm not sure I follow-"

"It's pretty simple," said Sophie curtly, finishing whatever it was she was typing then dropping her phone into her bag. She stared at her mother but said nothing. Carla knew she wasn't going to make it easy.

"Is she dating anyone ... similar?" said Carla at last, wondering if she was on the right track.

"Well, she's quivergender if that's what you mean."

Carla had never heard of quivergender.

"Actually," said Sophie thoughtfully. "I'd say they're both intersectional feminists now."

"Who? Linda - sorry I meant Linton?"

Sophie stared at her mother with contempt.

"I didn't mean I didn't follow as in *understand*," Carla said quickly, tweaking her place setting - a habit of hers - concentrating on unfolding the flimsy paper napkin and balancing it on her lap so that she didn't have to look at her daughter. "I meant it's just not an area I tend to follow."

There was a deadly silence.

"Never mind."

"No! I want to understand, really I do," said Carla now urgently. "I've always considered myself to be a - a feminist."

Sophie guffawed. "*You*?"

Carla nodded in an unconvincing manner. "But I don't think gender ever came into it."

They both were silent as Linda returned with a drink's menu.

"Forgot to give you this, ladies."

Carla didn't dare look at Linda's face in case Sophie accused her of staring. Instead, she was mesmerised by her large hands and long false nails. F-U-C-K was tattooed between the knuckles. One thing was certain; Carla was completely out of her comfort zone with all of this. Why weren't they at a nice Ivy chain restaurant sipping champagne surrounded by greenery Carla could actually recognise?

Sophie took a deep breath about to quiz Carla on her feminist views when she suddenly relaxed, appeased by the prospect of a drink. Carla looked away; she couldn't drink anyway as she was driving. Presumably, Sophie couldn't either unless she'd walked to work.

"Shall we share a cocktail?" It wasn't a question. "Look! They're doing two for one!" Sophie sounded positively elated.

"Even at lunchtime?" Carla regretted the words the minute they were out of her mouth.

"Yeah …"

"Do you think -?"

"What? You don't want one?"

The silence hung between them. A few sips, thought Carla, *I'll have a few sips if it buys harmony…*

"No, yes, yes, I'll have one," she said embarrassed at once by how incoherent she sounded. "What a good idea but you choose."

By the time the drinks came - two enormous fishbowls of an artificial raspberry flavoured liquid - the kind festooned with miniature parasols and straws that dissolved the minute they touched the tongue, Carla needed one. She took a quick gulp - peeling paper off her lips.

"Fuck, that's good," said Sophie.

Carla winced. *Did* she have to use such unladylike language?

"And getting back to what I was saying, maybe intersectional is the way to go, coz it's not just about gender."

Carla spluttered. "It's not?"

Sophie shook her head. "Sexuality, class, race and other intersections play a part. It's the way we live anyway. I mean there are hundreds out there now - trans female, or trans male, non-binary, polygender, staticgender-"

Carla somehow managed to slurp her drink. Her turn to be unladylike. She did hate paper straws - hers were a mess at the bottom of her glass, so she was forced to hold the enormous bowl to her mouth with both hands. There was no point in even trying to keep up - but if she didn't change the subject soon, everything was going to go pear-shaped - if it hadn't already.

"How's Cucumber?"

"*Cucumber?*" Amusement flitted across Sophie's face. "That's who you think of when we're discussing sexual politics?"

At the mention of her Labrador, Sophie's face softened with emotion, and a light came into her huge chocolate brown eyes. They were such innocent eyes, Carla felt a pang. An image came to her of Sophie when she was about eight years old, even younger than Alfie was now, crouched on their porch, a baby rabbit in her arms. Its fur had been very white against the scarlet of her school blazer. Sophie had held the rabbit with such sweetness, such gentleness. In much the same way, Carla held that image now, unpeeling the snapshot from the photograph album of memory to hold it gently against her heart. Was Carla responsible for the veneer of toughness that Sophie had adopted? Probably. Carla's eyes were moist. Sometimes her daughter's childhood seemed such a long time ago eclipsed by Alfie's more recent one. As Sophie talked on about Cucumber, Carla felt herself relax.

Baby steps. Maybe that's what it took, baby steps. She

shouldn't compare her relationship with Sophie to other peoples.' *Compare and despair.*' She should know better. It wasn't perfect, but whose fault was that? As long as she remembered that she, Carla, was responsible for this, then the small hurts shouldn't matter. Linda or Linton dropped their plates unceremoniously in front of them. Carla looked at her meal without appetite. Nothing to do with the service - this was the sort of place she loathed - the kind that pretended to be healthy but really wasn't. There was always too much dressing and lots of big white croutons.

"Looks great," said Sophie.

Carla smiled weakly, took another sip of her cocktail before picking up her fork. She took a bite of greasy looking chicken. Moments later, it felt as though Carla had swallowed paint stripper. First, the top of her mouth felt aflame and then her nostrils. She'd never taken drugs, never even had a puff of a cigarette, but she imagined this was what it must be like to have one's sinuses blown apart. She coughed, spluttered, begged Linton/Linda for some bread - anything to neutralise the burn.

Sophie's eyes narrowed. "It's not *that* hot."

"It is to me," Carla managed, at last, taking a swig of her cocktail.

Sophie's fork hovered over her plate. "Please," said Carla pushing her plate towards her daughter. "Be my guest."

When she'd finished, Sophie suddenly looked at her phone.

"I'm going to have to go," she said. "I told you I only get an hour." Sophie was fiddling with an eyebrow - she'd done this since she was little, twisting the fine hair.

"No, that's OK," said Carla. "I'll get this." She motioned to Linda, fishing out her lime green Hermès wallet. She'd purchased it after her first date with Seb. Elated, excited, already violently in love, she'd floated down Sloane Street and gone into the shop - bought it without looking at the price. Those were the days. Of complete foolishness.

"Sure?"

"Yes, of course."

Carla paid the bill and stood up to go, but Sophie remained seated. "You're never going to leave him, are you?" she said.

Carla sank back in her chair, feeling the familiar hand of dread, the tightening of her heart, the wiping of the happy mood. She made a helpless gesture, but there was no wriggle move with Sophie. She wasn't going to let things be.

"You said you'd leave - that when your rent was up on the last place - you'd leave."

"Did I?" She had. "I can't have left *two* husbands! That really would be careless," said Carla thinking of handbags and Wilde and hoping to make light of Sophie's comment. Again, she half rose in her seat, but Sophie wasn't going anywhere just yet.

"Can't you?"

"Well, obviously, I *could*. It's ... it's not so simple," said Carla feebly. "There's Alfie."

"So?"

"So ..." Carla didn't know what to say. Naively she supposed, she thought they'd moved on from all of that. She braced herself. "I also remember that you asked me once to promise I wouldn't do to Alfie what I'd done to you and Tom i.e. get a divorce."

Sophie stared at her. "Kids are tough. He'll get over it."

"Maybe, maybe not. Seb may be many things, but he's a good father. Besides," she said in a sad voice. "I thought you'd forgiven him."

"*I* did," said Sophie fiercely. "I just didn't expect you to."

*

Sophie's front door opened, and one of the ambulance men came out.

"She'll be fine," he said kindly. "She doesn't have a temperature and seems to be getting enough oxygen, but we're taking her in as a precaution."

"Thank you," said Carla, her voice jagged with emotion. "Thank you."

Behind him came Ed. Nothing had changed in that he still avoided meeting her eye. Next came Sophie, followed by the second ambulance man. She had a mask over her face and looked grey; a slight, fragile child, not a young woman. Instinctively, Carla rushed towards her, but Sophie took a step back, recoiling as though Carla were the one infected not the other way around.

"Best not," said the medic. "To be on the safe side."

"Yes, of course. Darling," she said to her daughter. "My poor love."

Sophie removed her mask, took a ragged breath. "Too late," she said, turning away from Carla. "Two days too late."

*

"How'd it go?" asked Seb coldly when she let herself into the house a couple of hours later. Too upset to go home directly, Carla had deliberately allowed herself to become entangled on the many spaghetti junctions around Portsmouth, going back on herself several times. She'd tried calling Tom, but he hadn't answered.

"Sophie's going to be fine," said Carla brightly. "And don't worry, I didn't touch her or anything. I wasn't allowed to! Besides I was standing on the opposite side of the street. The ambulance men said she didn't have a temperature so I don't think it can be the dreaded 'beeruus', but oh, Seb, her voice was so ragged."

"How could you tell her voice was ragged if you were standing where you said you were?"

"What?"

"I said, how could you tell? I mean you had to have been really close to know."

That night there was a frostiness between them. Carla lay in the comfort of their new bed, virtually floating on the air of their brand-new mattress. In all their time together, they'd never had a new bed. The old thing they'd inherited was so lumpy, the wooden slats beneath so flimsy, that Seb's every move created a trampoline effect. She rarely had a good night's sleep. Tonight, while part of her luxuriated in the new everything - their new house, the gorgeous new crisp White Company sheets, the Susie Watson bedside tables, the lovely lamps with their eau-de-nil silk shades, the scent of the narcissus she'd bought earlier, the other part was rigid with apprehension. Her physical body, cocooned on thousands of pounds worth of pocket springs, merely encased the tautness of her mental anguish.

The one thing no one told you about second marriages, she thought grimly was the grief generated by children from the first. And one of the issues was that their attitudes, the children's that is, were ever-changing - never fixed or constant. In her case, the twins never seemed to have entirely made up their mind about their step-parent. While Tom hadn't taken to Seb at the beginning, he tolerated him now albeit with a veneer of charm. Her son's innate good manners meant that he treated everyone - friend or foe - with the same aloof courtesy. *'Manners Makyth Man'* was certainly true in his case.

Sophie had liked Seb at the beginning, had found him amusing, and their love of horses had given them common ground. When Seb realised Tom missed Angus, he'd made a conscious decision to spend more time with him. Sophie had reacted badly. Carla realised then that her daughter's initial jealousy of Tom (not something she'd expected of twins) was total. It wasn't that as a mother, Carla could have divided her time between her children equally. If you loved Sophie, then Sophie demanded 100% of you, anything less was a betrayal. But that wasn't the whole story. Of course, it wasn't. And now, the extent of Sophie's dislike was made all the more confusing to Carla because she never failed to give Seb a present at Christmas or a card on his birthday.

Seb had begun to snore - this was a recent development - his snoring. In the early days of their relationship, Carla had been smug when her girl-friends complained about their partners and the fact that some of them played musical beds at night caused by interrupted and/or sleepless nights. That was not one of their issues - making love through the night did cause sleepy days, but it wasn't because of Seb's snoring. Then he'd been fit - riding twice a week, maintaining a strict diet - in fact so strict a diet that she, who had always eaten healthily anyway, found herself sneaking out to Harvey Nichols (Seb lived in Eaton Square in those days) and buying exorbitantly expensive biscuits to snack on. Now the sound of his *breathing* kept her awake at night, let alone anything else.

Carla *should* have gone straight to Sophie when she returned. She should have. But then, what if Sophie had had the dreaded virus after all? She might have infected Alfie and Seb and anyone else they'd come into contact with since they came home. Or was it a risk she should have taken? As the loving mother, Sophie needed her to be? But it didn't mean Carla loved her less. Carla felt the cool sheet beneath her. She was so tired of always having to choose between Seb and the twins. That was one thing, Seb could never understand. And as far as Sophie was concerned, Carla had chosen Seb over her. That was the crux of it, and Carla was pretty sure it was the reason Sophie still wanted Carla to leave Seb, to show the world that Carla chose Sophie over and above every other living person. That was how her daughter would always see this. Carla had been naïve if she thought that somehow all those years ago, a line had been drawn that they would never revisit what had happened or that Sophie wouldn't continue to do so as long as she lived.

Tell him I'll forgive him, Sophie had said *if* ....

And she, Carla, had been so eager, so desperate for her world (which had been rocked off its axel within minutes) to be steadied, to go back to what it was, that she had readily agreed. Furthermore, in what she had believed to be the ultimate expression of trust, Carla had never asked for details, had never known exactly. Therefore, if Sophie could forgive Seb, then couldn't she? Hers was a second marriage - a short marriage in comparison to the one she'd had with Angus. She couldn't fail. And there was Alfie - beautiful Alfie. The product of their love - hers at any rate. They'd drawn a truce and Sophie had gone off to her boarding school in Scotland accompanied by not one but two horses - the cost of which amounted to having another child in full-time education. Neither parent had batted an eyelid. Carla hadn't, prompted by guilt and nor had Angus, anxious as he was to finalise their divorce.

The bedroom wasn't quite dark, and Carla could see the black and white photograph of the twins on her bedside table. They'd been about three years old at the time, seated on a white rattan garden chair wearing matching sailor suits. Both the chair and the stripes of their clothing were particularly suited to being shot in monochrome. The picture was timeless and beautiful. The twins were glancing down, smiling, still, yet somehow in motion, their blonde hair blowing in an imagined breeze. Tom had Sophie's bare little foot in his hand. But you sensed that at any given moment a tug too hard on those adorable little toes and one twin would wallop the other. All Carla wished now, was that she had gathered both babies in her arms and held them together, that she could now. Had she ever? One at a time, perhaps? But together?

Carla's phone hidden under a copy of *The Spectator* lit up her corner of the room.

Sorry for being so horrible. I love you.

Carla strangled a sob in the softness of her 100% Siberian pillow, touched the photograph with a kiss and fell instantly asleep.

6

She could feel him pushing against her, a kiss dropped on her naked shoulder, the roughness of his unshaven cheek. It was easier to acquiesce. Later Seb was cheerful. *'How's my beautiful girl?'* He'd said cupping her face in his hands, legs planted. Possessively. *You are mine, mine* emanating from every bit of him. Breathless, eager not to revert to their pole positions of the previous day, she had smiled though she'd wanted to say *How d'you think I feel? Sophie's in hospital, and I can't see her. And not because she won't see me, but now it's because I'm not allowed to see her!* Of course, she knew he was secretly thrilled that hospital visits were banned, thereby reducing any risk to him of infection.

"Come on, let's go and grab a coffee. I think some places are doing takeaways. Alfie's still asleep. We'll let him lie in. Get him a bacon bap from Nero - he'll enjoy that."

Carla nodded. It was hard to digest the speed with which the world - her world was changing. They'd only left the country a couple of weeks before: a house they'd only just moved into, a diary crammed with fun events far into the future - save- the-dates here, big birthday celebrations there. And school. Boarding school for Alfie. Now, it looked as though much of that wouldn't happen. It felt surreal, incredible, as though at any moment she'd wake up from this - well it wasn't exactly a nightmare, at least not yet - but certainly an altered reality.

"The good news," said Seb clasping her hand tightly as they walked past an unnervingly silent cathedral to an all but deserted high street. "Is that *statistically*, around 51,000 people die in Britain during any given month. At the moment there are some 422 deaths linked with Covid-19, so that's 0.8 per cent of the expected total. These figures might increase, but right now they're lower than that of other infectious diseases that we live with - such as flu."

Carla nodded. She hated when he got pedantic about a subject - this new virus was fast becoming it. "See," she said. In a 'told you so' tone. *Wasn't that what I said the other day? Except the deaths were rising...*

Seb ignored her. "If the cases increase exponentially say jumping from 5 to 15 per cent as they've done in China and Italy, then no healthcare in the world could cope with the prospect of that death rate."

"So, the objective will be to slow the rate of infection, so our NHS can cope -"

"Exactly."

"But then again many people may die. I *know* that it's affecting older people with underlying health conditions who might have died anyway. I mean, how will they *know* that it was the Corona by itself that was the cause of death, as opposed to the something else, with Corona."

"Yes, but if they'd not had Corona, they'd not have died."

"Yeah, but that applies to pneumonia or flu. A person can have cancer, but it will be something else that ultimately kills them. Presumably, if we tracked flu or other seasonal viruses, there'd also be an exponential increase, and we'd be freaked."

Seb had thought of something else. He dropped her hand, ran his own through his hair.

"Well, in my case," he said gloomily. "It's Russian Roulette - a one in three chance that I'll die."

Carla raised her eyes. *Give me strength!* "Or a 66% chance that you'll live," she said brightly.

They'd reached the 14th century Butter Cross. Tourist information gave out that the stone statue was covered in twelve figures, but Carla could only ever make out two. Traditionally, it was where dairy products were sold to the good people of the city. Today, not even pigeons chose to perch on its slippery slope, as if instinctively knowing to keep a distance. A handful of places were still open to supplying sandwiches and coffee, but the rest of the High Street was empty. Others announced their imminent closure due to the spread of Covid.

That most quintessential of English shops, Laura Ashely, was also closing its doors, although in its case for the last time. Carla was sad they were folding although she couldn't say she'd ever loved their clothes. Her first husband had liked her in Laura Ashely smocks, but that was because they reminded him of his mother. She'd *felt* like Lady Annabel wearing those shapeless floral sacks. In middle-age, her former mother-in-law had lost herself in India, doggedly traipsing around the world after Bhagwan Shree Rajneeh only to be disillusioned when the man who became infamous as the sex cult guru, advised her to have it off (she pronounced it orff) with as many people as possible. To the family's relief, she had re-found herself in a gentler environment in California, with an even gentler colour consultant called Carole, who dressed them both head to toe in lilac.

Carla waited in front of the chocolate shop on the corner. It was even quieter than Christmas Day. Or maybe it was just her imagination. The early morning sun had disappeared, and the wind was up spreading clouds in a jagged line across the pale sky.

Seb held out a cappuccino.

"Ah, thanks."

"I do love you, you know."

She murmured something, her response swallowed by the froth on her upper lip. But she felt an inner glow all the same.

Harmoniously, they retraced their steps passing the William Walker pub. Carla often wondered how many people spared a thought for its namesake, the deep-sea diver who for six years had worked underwater and in total darkness to secure the foundations of the east end of the Cathedral. Then again, there were so many unsung heroes who went about their daily jobs quietly, stoically. Walking through the crooked slype, they were about to encounter one more.

There was a sudden darkening of the skies and an unearthly, menacing silence. And then just as they passed under the carved hand that directed worshippers to one side, walkers to the other, they could hear someone playing the accordion. As in a film, the delicate strands of *Somewhere Over the Rainbow* teased them forward, reawakening with exquisite nostalgia, the flutterings of desire, the yearning for something more. If *that* hadn't happened, how would she feel now? She glanced at Seb in profile - the right profile, the one that was virile and irresistible, the man she'd fallen head-over-heels in love with. The man she'd have left everything for, *had* left everything for. They walked on. The musician revealed himself, a middle-aged, handsome Slav, with a face full of humanity and a cigarette dangling from the corner of his mouth. He seemed oblivious of the cold bitter wind, concentrating only on imparting this gesture of solidarity, this small precious gift. Carla felt tears prick her eyes. She clapped. He acknowledged her with an almost imperceptible nod which was enough for Seb's fingers to clamp down tight. Enough for the moment of desire on her part, to pass.

Alfie was still asleep when they got home. There seemed little point in waking him, besides which, Carla could do with a few hours to herself. At least she could look forward to Evensong in the Cathedral later in the day. She'd catch up with some of the other mothers. They wouldn't - couldn't sit too close even if they'd wanted to - the 14th-century oak choir stalls were capacious, all-enclosing. She loved leaning back, hidden from the rest of the attendants and studying the human figures, carved animals and foliage on the backs of the pews and columns. She tried to sit directly under the exquisitely painted ceiling panel, through which a bell was lowered on feast days. All around, ogee arches soared upwards on cusped heads, taking with them the stresses of the day. What would she wear? After the heat of Cartagena, she was feeling the cold even more keenly. Navy blue, she decided - her go-to Max Mara and new Christian Dior handbag. Boots or flats? Maybe flats seeing as it was technically spring.

Carla went up to her dressing room - in effect a walk-in wardrobe - meticulously catalogued according to brand, season and colour. She'd had her clothes moved separately over three days before they left on holiday, not trusting them to the general household movers. She was glad she had. Carla flipped through colour co-ordinated cashmere, jeans, wide-legged wool pants, Gucci blouses, figure-hugging DVF dresses, dozens of Prada jumpsuits for winter and summer, and row upon row up of shoes. She settled on a pair of Alice brand leather pants and a Céline blouse. Stripping down to her underwear, she noted with pleasure how tanned her body was from their holiday and how well she felt from days in the sun. How long ago it already seemed! She wished now, that she'd swum more, got up earlier, held on to those moments of contentment - the feel of Seb's fingers trailing her skin. It was beginning to be a bit of a blur. She removed her diamond studs, replacing them with Mikimoto pearl drops. Still not a sound from Alfie.

Seb met her on the landing. He was wearing the wool gilet they'd bought in Aguascalientes a few months before. Over the past eighteen months they'd visited South America four times. It had taken Carla forty years to visit the continent and now she couldn't get enough of the place. Since the previous September, they'd been to Chile, Argentina, Easter Island, Brazil, Panama and Colombia. And of course, Peru. Carla had become practised in rattling off the list of countries when asked if they'd been 'anywhere nice' recently. After all, she wasn't on her 'gap yah'. But as she reminded her girlfriends, the twins were adults now, in full-time employment. Only Alfie was still of school age, and he boarded. Now was 'their' time, she said. She'd spent the whole of her first marriage stuck at home, not even taking the twins on bucket and spade holidays to Cornwall. She wasn't waiting any longer. What she didn't say, was that travelling with Seb was when she could completely forget what had happened, could pretend that they were still madly in love, that second-time marriages were worth all the grief and upheaval, that he - especially when they were far away - was home, that there was nowhere else she'd rather be.

Aguascalientes had almost put paid to that. When they arrived in Cusco, they had already travelled the length of Chile and Argentina. Carla had loved Santiago the year before when they'd visited on their way to Easter Island, which had proven to be a whole other adventure in itself. On that occasion, they'd been stranded in Rapa Nui for an extra week due to bad weather. She was surprised at how much she'd enjoyed the sense of isolation, the feeling of comradery with all the other tourists they'd bumped into, some more desperate than others to leave the island. Carla had even loved their simple room, no more than a converted garage space, but warm and inviting after a day crisscrossing the island in stormy weather. They'd tried to take in as many Moai as possible (there were almost a thousand) from the Tongariki in the palm-fringed sandy alcove to the majestic statues standing sentinel at Ahu Akivi.

Most recently, they'd once again passed through Santiago, spending a single night in the delectable Singular Hotel - fast becoming one of Carla's all-time favourites - before flying down to Punta Arenas the next morning. Carla had found the whole trip deeply romantic. Sandy Point (in English), was the furthest, southern city in the world and the largest south of the 46th parallel. Even now, Carla had a vision of Seb pouring over the map of the Magellan Straits, his phone buzzing him with the message: *You're a long way from home.*

It had felt wonderfully, isolating (little did she know what that word would *really* come to mean), adventurous and brave, although nothing remotely comparable to what real explorers had endured. Everywhere was evidence of truly marvellous expeditions - a plaque on the wall of the British Club commemorated Shackleton's successful bid to rescue his men stranded on Elephant Island. With such invigorating tales of heroism pumping adrenaline through her every artery, they'd travelled by road to Puerto Natales and from there by boat to the Balmaceda river and glacier. Shivering in bright sunshine, they'd seen the Torres del Paine - sharp icicle peaks, upended against a dazzling azure sky. Carla had taken deep breaths of the pure, freezing air and felt refreshed, reinvigorated ready to keep going - to keep trying.

The final leg of that journey had taken them to a misty, foggy and slightly chilly Lima. With rain dripping over the glass partition of the Observatory Restaurant, they had bravely sipped cocktails and pretended it wasn't nearly as cold as it felt. Seb pointed out that Carla, in blue and taupe Balmain, blended perfectly against the backdrop of potted purple hydrangeas. Carla, for her part, was lulled by the mesmerising power - a particular hypnotic ferocity of the Pacific - as it crashed along the length of the Miraflores coastline.

It was reminiscent of that other dramatic panorama: Rio and Carla remembered being awed by the majestic, vast landscape of that glorious city. From the Corcovado Mountain, they had watched the sunrise - the light streaming in rainbow ribbons like a halo around Sugarloaf and the Guanabara Bay. But watch was all they could do. They'd been so terrified by the warnings of street crime (a girlfriend advised tying up her hair as robbers were going about lopping off European locks to sell for wigs) that they'd decided to leave their phones behind. It didn't matter; the memory of that morning was engraved on her heart.

Earlier in Lima, they'd clambered over the book-like structures of Huaca Pucllana, that adobe pyramid to be found in the heart of the city. Then thoroughly tired after crossing Kennedy Park, they'd stopped at Lucha Sangucheria for melt-in-your-mouth sandwiches like none Carla had ever tasted - hot, white crispy rolls piled high with roast chicken, lettuce - or whatever topping you fancied.

"There's one more place I'd like to see before we head back," Carla had said after they'd finished their coffee and she knew Seb was feeling sated.

"Sure." One of the many things that Carla always appreciated about Seb was his willingness to do (virtually) anything she suggested. Her ex had been a 'no' man.

"Follow me," she directed, surreptitiously glancing at her guide book. She had an appalling sense of direction but never liked Seb to know just how bad it really was. "Yes, of course, I'm sure," she added, feeling his unease as she headed purposefully across the Plaza de Armas.

"I know it's here," muttered Carla as wide avenues gave way to narrow streets and they finally emerged onto Calle Jirón de La Unión. "It says that Casa Aliaga is the oldest Colonial mansion," she peered closely at a grainy photograph that looked nothing like the houses they'd seen so far, "not only in Peru but the whole of South America - that the first de Aliaga, arrived from Sanlúcar in the 16th century." She looked up eyes dancing. "I've been there! Sanlúcar I mean." She adjusted her cashmere cardigan. It really was freezing.

In contrast, she recalled a holiday dominated by blistering heat. Cadiz, at the height of an August summer, was fly-blown and dusty; all the beautiful squares and plazas as described in the guidebooks had seen better days - better *centuries* - clearly, the time when Jeronimo de Aliaga set sail for Panama and the Americas. She loved that phrase, 'the Americas' - it always sounded so romantic. Her fascination with the place had started then, however subliminally. Tingling with excitement, Carla came to a stop in front of an unprepossessing looking house with an intricate *mirador* or wooden balcony - those Spanish/Moorish influenced outdoor rooms designed to allow women of the nobility a chance to view the city without themselves being seen. Carla remembered a play by Mario Vargas Llosa called *The Madman of the Balconies*. She mentioned this to Seb, but he looked puzzled.

"I thought you said the balconies were for *women*."

"Yes," she agreed, "they were, but I think the play was about a man who was on a campaign to *restore* them." She couldn't actually remember the story in any detail. She'd read Vargas Llosa once upon a time when she was trying to improve her Spanish. She'd almost bumped into the Nobel Prize winner and future Presidential Candidate, strolling near Pandora, a shop that sold pre-loved designer clothes in Knightsbridge. He'd been living in London at the time. She wished now that she'd been brave enough to speak to him.

Above the massive bronze knocker on the double-fronted door of the Casa Aliaga was an even larger embossed coat of arms - a warning to interlopers. But the owner welcomed them warmly telling them to make themselves at home - (*'mi casa es su casa'*) to wander where they liked. They stepped over the high threshold (devised initially to keep mud and debris from the street) and into a courtyard larger than Carla's first flat. But unlike the stone courtyards with which Carla was familiar, this one was made entirely of wood with a glossy ebony sheen.

Directly ahead was a straight, wide staircase. Carla wasted no time in vaulting ahead of Seb, wanting to be the first to explore the upstairs rooms. She loved nothing better than to visit old houses infused with the romanticism of a bygone era. She was not disappointed. An innocuous, slightly dilapidated exterior, concealed a mansion crammed with gilt furniture, china, occasional tables, heavy drapes and tapestries. Different rooms boasted different styles - French baroque to Viceregal. Others were made up entirely of *azulejos* or the Spanish/Moorish tiles which were not only decorative but devised to control the temperature. Carla wondered how exactly. Apart from Chilean Patagonia, this was the coldest she'd been during their entire time in South America.

Seb paused before yet another engraved coat of arms. They were everywhere, above every door frame, picture and used on wallpaper and fabric.

"There's no forgetting who owns this place," he said wryly.

"I suppose," said Carla peering at row upon row of family portraits, "it's not every day you have sixteen consecutive generations living in the same house."

"Unless you're royalty."

Carla had her back to the Gold Room with its Louis XIV furniture, delicate legs atop skating rink slippery parquet flooring. She glanced up at the mezzanine with its display of Japanese vases. In all, there were sixty-six rooms including, a Neo-Gothic chapel.

"I think being the 18th Count de Aliaga is as good as." She examined several silver-framed photos of the King of Spain, Vargas Llosa and famous film stars. "The first de Aliaga came to Peru with Francisco Pizarro. He was one of *los trece de fama* - the famous 13."

"Famous for what?"

She could tell Seb was becoming bored. He had begun

chewing on his pen - always a bad sign.

"Well," said Carla injecting enthusiasm into her voice. "When Pizarro was waiting on the Isla del Gallo for bad weather to clear, he drew a line in the sand with his sword. He said, 'those on that side of the line can return to Panama and be poor, those on this side can continue on to Peru with me and become rich.'"

Seb patted an ornate finial. "He made the right decision. By the way, where is the Isla del Gallo?"

That night in San Isidro, they had drinks with a university friend of Carla's someone she'd not seen in ..? They were gathered around a low table in a dark, black faux-suede box of a bar trying to count.

"Must be thirty years."

"No!"

"Yes!"

Diego sat back in the velveteen hub of his chair. Seb sat forward in his. He had trouble hearing. Background noise was always problematic, and Diego spoke very softly.

"So, what have you seen? The cathedral with its unusual picture of the last supper?"

Carla nodded. Unusual it certainly was. The picture of *The Last Supper* by Marcos Zapata was a perfect clash of Latin American versus European culture. Jesus was depicted contemplating a meal of roasted guinea pig, its legs sticking straight up.

"And the Casa d'Aliaga of course."

"Of course."

"You know that up to 100 people would have lived in the house in Pizarro's time?"

Carla shook her head. Diego took a sip of his white wine. Seb was drinking water, and she'd ordered a Pisco Sour which she was fast regretting. It was delicious but too strong, and already her head had begun to throb. The music was deafening, and she had to lean towards him and away from Seb to hear him speak.

"Apparently, the servants slept standing upright."

"Tolstoy's servants would do the same."

"*Tolstoy?*" Seb had heard that perfectly. It amused him that her references were never particularly modern.

Carla swivelled to her husband.

"Yes, Tolstoy. When his bride arrived at Yasanya Polyana, his country estate, she was shocked at how he lived. Actually, she was shocked about a lot of things, but she didn't like that his servants would fall asleep where they dropped with fatigue. After she arrived she made sure they all had beds."

"What was she called?" There was an edge to his tone.

"Who?"

"Tolstoy's wife?"

Carla made an impatient gesture. "Sophia." *Where was he going with this?* she wondered. *That wasn't the point of the story…*

"Ah yes," said Diego thoughtfully, "I remember now. You

liked Russian, didn't you? You were even in Russia when we were supposed to be sitting our first-year history exams."

"Really?" said Seb. "I didn't know that about you."

Carla shrugged. There were lots of things Seb didn't know, not really. He was so jealous of her past that she'd found it easier not to tell him anything, even the things she would like to have shared with him. There was a further moment of tenseness.

"Ah, but this was different," said Diego quickly. "The servants slept in the narrow spaces *between* the walls. At night, the owners locked them in, because, although they depended on the indigenous people, they were also afraid of them. The Spaniards were outnumbered, and they knew that any uprising would mean their death."

"That's awful," said Carla.

Diego finished his drink.

"Another?" offered Seb gallantly. Carla smiled at him, gratefully and the hostile moment between them passed. "And it's on us by the way."

"No way," said Diego, a phrase he repeated throughout the evening like a *refrán* to one of the songs he used to strum on his guitar. As the evening wore on, it became increasingly difficult to equate the middle-age Diego with the skinny, dark-haired Peruvian aristocrat of yesteryear. He'd been unbelievably cool then. While the rest of their classmates lived in dodgy digs, Diego had an entire house in Kensington at his disposal. He was a prince (his mother was a Lithuanian princess) and his sister had dated Eric Clapton.

He also sweated profusely although Carla found it cold in the air-conditioned night club. She chattered on hurtling from one subject to the next. When they left, Carla felt wistful. Not for their student time again but for the promise of the future that was theirs. It made her question what exactly she had done with hers. Like Diego, she also had two marriages under her belt, although in her case, both her husbands were very much alive. She had a History degree, three children but no job - unless you counted a few hours here and there translating inane questions for Spanish speaking young offenders (*'hay un Mcdonalds?'* and *'puedo llamar a casa?'*). The only real way she stretched her brain these days was by planning ever more complicated travel routes for their extended holidays, hence the patchwork approach to air travel through Latin America.

Which is why they were now headed to Cusco, one of the highest cities in the world. The Captain of their boat in the Galapagos, who also happened to be a pilot with Avianca, had told them that the approach to Cusco airport was also one of the most hazardous. Along with horror stories of near-accidents (Carla was amazed they'd ever thought to fly again), Tobias told them to make sure they arrived by 10 a.m. at the latest. Carla had dutifully followed his advice and chosen the first flight of the day. Bleary-eyed they'd arrived at the terminus with Seb insisting on finding an Uber - always a frantic endeavour with intermittent Wi-Fi, and invariably ending with him stomping off and leaving her with the luggage.

At last they'd arrived at the Belmond Monasterio, a 16th-century former monastery built on the foundations of Amaru Qhala's Inca palace whose tall walls and grandiose wooden portals belied the charm of the place within. Standing in the open lobby, a brisk breeze rustling the odd leaf across the cobblestones, Carla felt herself carefully unwind as though every part of her - complex mechanism that she was - had to be disassembled in precise order. Through graceful arches, she glimpsed vibrant Cusco art: paintings in gold, red and ochre depicting images of the Holy Family against a foreground of Peruvian flora and fauna.

Feeling drowsy, they'd decided to have a coffee before going up to their room. The cloistered courtyard was inviting with huge parasols surrounded by potted plants - roses and birds of paradise.

"*Strelizia reginae*," she'd said touching the flower's fan-shaped crown and sinking gratefully into a padded chair.

"Come again," said Seb.

"Also known as the crane flower," she pointed to the white and blue nectary. "See, when sunbirds drink its nectar the petals open to cover their feet in pollen."

Seb shook his head in amazement. "The stuff you come up with. But 'reginae'? Of the queen - I know that much Latin. What's the other word? What does it mean?"

"It's the name of George III's wife. Charlotte of Mecklenburg-Streliz."

"Yeah, think I prefer 'crane flower'."

Seb felt the sharp, beak-like sheath with the tip of his finger and then pulled it back quickly.

Carla shook her head. "You don't have to worry. It doesn't produce any air-borne pollen. You won't be allergic."

Seb looked at her in wonder. "It's amazing what you know."

Carla flushed, pleased. "It's not really. You forget, I used to do translation for pharmaceutical companies."

"But knowing, *remembering* the Charlotte bit?"

"History *and* pharma - just up my street." As if on cue, a bird came to settle above the long green stalk. "It's also the official flower of the City of Los Angeles. And," she looked away, "the flowers are slow-growing and won't bloom until three to five years have passed since germination. They only really flower when they are properly established ..."

Her voice faded. Was that true too of forgiveness, she wondered. How long would it really take before the bloom of hers was creamy and unspoiled and true? She knew that there was one variety called 'Mandela's Gold.' *He* had been able to forgive.

Carla was quiet until their coffee arrived, enjoying the sun on her face, the warmth after chilly Lima. Seb also closed his eyes, his hands in his pockets, his legs outstretched. Afterwards, she'd unpacked her suitcase, pausing to flick through a guide to the hotel facilities and noting with amusement that the top floor boasted an 'Oxygen Room.' Seb reminded Carla that Cusco had an elevation of 3,399 metres. If she wasn't feeling it already, altitude sickness was often a negative health effect. So far, she'd felt fine and was just eager to be out. She changed her clothes picking out a pretty silk Prada dress (pink lips on a white background print) which had prompted Seb to hum *'Bésame Mucho'*) and headed for the beauty salon. After having the Valley of the Moon sand washed out of her hair and nails, she was ready for sightseeing.

They'd then spent a long, lovely afternoon at Sacsahuaman, the Inca citadel towards the north of the city, its complex of stones a taster of what they would see at Machu Pichu. As evening fell, they retraced their steps to the Plaza de Armas with its imposing statue of Pachacutec, the 9th Sapa ruler, and headed to the Hiram Bingham museum. Carla was captivated by the story of the Yale history lecturer who having read about the four-hundred-year-old mystery concerning a lost city, its inhabitants and the vast treasure of an Empire was determined to find it. Carla imagined the handsome Bingham, impeccably dressed in old-fashioned riding britches staring at the impenetrable cloud forest and wondering where to begin. Deploying his considerable personal fortune to outfitting his expedition with the most up-to-date scientific instruments available at the time, and himself (the character of Indiana Jones was modelled on him), he set out to find the legendary Vilcabamba. What he stumbled upon instead was the geometric splendour of Machu Pichu. Except that Machu Pichu wasn't the only ruin he 'discovered.' In the course of his three expeditions to Peru, he had 'found' the mountaintop citadel of Choquequirao, the holy shrine at Vitcos and the jungle city Espiritu Pampa.

Seb was more interested in the continuing controversy concerning Bingham's discovery. A former First Lady of Peru demanded that Yale return the artefacts Bingham had excavated in her country. She referred to him not, as an explorer but a *huaquero* - grave robber.

Carla shrugged this off. "What's a few knick-knacks?"

Seb looked up from one of the exhibits.

"40,000 bone fragments and specimens aren't 'a few knick-knacks', and Bingham knew what he was doing. Even in 1911 or whenever it was, the Peruvian Government didn't allow archaeological finds to be removed from its country."

"Oh, come on!" said Carla "Museums everywhere are full to

bursting with antiquities garnered from all over the world by wealthy 'travellers.' Look at the Louvre or our very own British Museum!"

"True," agreed Seb evenly. "And you're right. Up until Bingham began his excavations, artefacts had passed out of the country unchecked. But because he was already such a public figure and there was so much publicity surrounding his expedition, Peruvians began to rethink their whole attitude towards its heritage and preserving their indigenous treasures. Ironically, the same man who invited Bingham to witness his excavation (with explosives!), later forbade him from undertaking more."

"Which Bingham ignored."

"Which Bingham ignored. Happily, for us."

Carla studied a photograph of the explorer. Even in black and white, his eyes were penetrating and intense.

"I would still argue that Bingham didn't *steal* the artefacts. He purchased them in good faith. Besides, locals had ransacked the place already over the years."

"Maybe, maybe not. Doesn't make what Bingham did right."

"Well, it does if he was only purchasing stuff that was for sale in the first place, if he bought it in good faith."

"I'm sure it was never that."

Carla was annoyed he was casting doubt on her hero.

"We don't know."

Seb said nothing for a moment, prowling through the small rooms, barely stopping to see the exhibits and speed reading the accompanying text. Despite his short attention span, he always managed to cut to the chase.

"Interesting that early on, Yale and Peru enjoyed quite a good relationship. They were even planning on opening a new museum *together*."

"Yeah, I read that. Instead they ended up suing each other."

"And," said Seb gleefully, "did you read the bit where the bones that Bingham discovered in 1912 which he thought dated back to the Ice Age, turned out to be those of a domestic cow?"

"Yes," said Carla tightly. "I read that too."

She was in no doubt as to whose side she was on. Still, they continued to debate the issue as they walked towards the Plazoleta Nazarenas and over supper at La Bodega - a cute Italian bistro a hundred yards from their hotel serving thick chicken soup and gallons of coca tea - both useful for combatting altitude sickness. They agreed on some elements of Bingham's dazzling story - hundreds of photographs doing more to convey the magic of the Andes, the extraordinary precision of Inca masonry - than the explorer's own words ever could. Amazingly, Bingham's micro-managed account concentrated more on lists of maladies suffered by members of the expedition - he had a peculiar fascination for lists in general - rather than on the fantastic discovery itself.

But a dull headache (despite or perhaps because of the gallons of coca tea she'd drunk at supper) had set in, and soon they were heading back to the oasis of the hotel, happy that they had long passed the back-packer stage and could look forward to crisp linen sheets, hot showers and fluffy towels. Carla tried to read. She alternated Mark Adam's

Turn Right at Machu Pichu with Vargas Llosa's *Death in the Andes* but felt too nauseous to concentrate. The 'Oxygen Room,' she discovered too late, was no gimmick.

However, in the morning, excitement replaced the last vestiges of nausea. The air was bracing as Carla ambled down long, stone corridors. Wide beams of sunlight set crimson runners ablaze, yellow-painted walls a kaleidoscope of colour. Triangles of dazzling azure sky segmented open cloisters, as Carla hurried to meet Seb who had gone on ahead. Breakfast was set up in the central courtyard under a three-hundred-year-old cedar tree. Carla paused, waiting to be seated, although she could see her husband perfectly clearly. She enjoyed the admiring glances and knew she looked good in her beige slacks, apricot nubuck Tods and Pucci blouse. A vicuña cashmere wrap she'd bought somewhere in San Blas - the city's artists' quarter - was draped over her shoulders. She repeatedly popped on her Panama hat (the one Seb had bought for her at the Montecristo shop in Quito) and took it off again, in case it flattened her hair. She juggled the danger of burning with the vanity of looking good.

"Wear it," said Seb acknowledging her arrival by briefly rising in his chair, in much the same way he would if he were half rising in the trot. "You don't want wrinkly skin."

It was only afterwards, when Carla turned over their every conversation in her head, that she realised Seb's reserve started then, at breakfast. Later, when she looked back at that morning, she marvelled that she hadn't read the signs which now in retrospect, were as clear as that radiant day. At the time, Carla quietened pinpricks of anxiety, those tingles of unease that if allowed, could easily mutate to the scratchiness that often existed between them. She wasn't going to let anything - especially not his silences (because she could chat for both of them) - to spoil this day - a day she'd looked forward to ever since she was a young girl. But it wasn't just reading about explorers that had ignited her interest in Machu Pichu. First learning about the mighty Urubamba and the resting place of Inca nobility, Ollantaytambo, had long fired her romantic imagination. Everything so far about Cusco was dreamy - well they'd not had sex, but she put that down to altitude sickness, hers as much as his. Seb was tactile enough, continually reaching for her hand, grabbing her as she walked past, telling her he liked her cheekbones. Did that mean she was getting old she thought in a moment's panic? She folded that thought away just as she folded herself into the waiting taxi, immaculate and refreshed with their neat carry-ons, before arriving at the train station - 3,486 metres above sea level. She wouldn't remind Seb how high they were or he'd start feeling the altitude.

"Funny name," he volunteered as they alighted, reading the district sign. "'Poroy'."

Carla could answer this. "It's a corruption of the Spanish *por hoy* - 'for today.' Early Spaniards would rest here 'for today' on their way to Cusco."

Seb nodded. "Makes sense."

"And now," continued Carla, her voice cracking with emotion, "we're about to follow the same route that Hiram Bingham did over a hundred years ago!"

"There it is," said Seb. Truncated sections of the blue and gold 1920's style Pullman carriages could be glimpsed through the waiting area. Dancers in colourful swirling skirts, embroidered waistcoats and strange red headdresses (kerchiefs with an added topknot) and musicians wearing the typical poncho poured onto the platform. Champagne was served, although it was only 9 a.m. Carla didn't care - she was too jagged with jet lag and excitement to exert any self-control. Gratefully, she accepted a drink, taking a quick sip before setting her glass down on a flimsy table which had been hastily erected under a green awning. The music had started up, and one of the dancers asked her to dance. She whirled and twirled already feeling tipsy, joyously living in the moment. For once, Seb didn't seem to mind her dancing with another man. He usually was jealous if anyone looked at her longer than he thought appropriate; now he positively encouraged her. Confused by his reaction, Carla stopped short, catching her husband by the arm to encourage him to dance with her. Seb was an accomplished dancer. He could ballroom dance like a pro, but whether he felt self-conscious dancing on a platform in front of a waiting train, Carla couldn't tell. He wasn't normally shy. But she wasn't going to let his reluctance to join in, pierce her mood. What she needed was another drink.

The table under the green awning now struggled to accommodate so many empty glasses. Carla was certain she'd left hers, by another covered in lipstick.

"Ah, no, Señorita," said a stranger. "I believe that one is mine."

Carla's hand flew to her mouth in exaggerated horror. "Oh, no! I'm so sorry!" she said. "I'm so sorry!"

The man smiled.

"Jaime," he said. "*Aqui para servirle.*"

Carla loved that expression - 'at your service' - common in Latin America but not used so much in Spain. And obviously, it *sounded* better in Spanish. It seemed quaint to her, oldie worldie. This Jaime also managed to spark something of the old Seb in him because he was by her side in an instance.

"Ah," said Jaime. "The boyfriend?"

"The husband," said Seb grimly, bowing curtly. Carla knew that people unfamiliar with his mannerisms, might have mistaken the greeting as a courtesy. Carla knew it was more of a 'good-bye 'than 'hello.' She hid a smile.

"And I'm Carla. You're from here?" she added in Spanish noting the man's slight accent, his Spanish name.

Jaime bowed himself this time. "Colombia. I am Colombian. But you are Spanish *verdad*?"

Both their accents immediately placed them in different continents. Seb pressed her hand possessively for a moment.

Jaime turned away, taking his glass with him. "Enjoy your trip."

And then he hesitated, leaning to whisper in her ear. "You really are the most elegant woman on this train."

Carla hesitated only briefly before leaning to his other.

"I know."

And then they were being ushered slickly along the platform to their compartments then up three short steps to their elegant tables. Origami-stiff table cloths displayed slender vases of orchids (there were three thousand varieties to be found in Peru - four hundred in Machu Pichu alone) and fresh glasses of ice-cold champagne. Settling into her plush seat, Carla purred inwardly with pleasure. It was a pleasure that was heightened by the frisson of Jaime's compliment, the delight in their lush, spacious surroundings, of being with a man (if she could forget what had happened), was the only man she had ever truly loved. And just for today, she told herself, for this one day she *would* forget - she would pretend that they had triumphed against the odds, that they had a future, that they were happy.

She smiled across the table.

"Here we are *mi amor*, here we are."

After a lunch sourced entirely from the various communities to be found in the Sacred Valley - salt from the mines of Pichingoto and maise from Huayllabamba, the train rumbled through the Potomales gorge. Ahead, the snow-capped peak of the five thousand, seven hundred metres-high Veronica Mountain suddenly came into view and then just as quickly disappeared. Leaving Seb to snooze in their cabin, Carla walked the length of the train to the observation carriage where gusts of hot, dusty air soon cooled as they crossed from Andean highland to lush cloud forest and jungle.

From time to time there was a cry of excitement amongst the guests at the sighting of a condor or the national bird of Peru the *Gallito de las Rocas* (Cock of the Rocks) easily identified by its red-orange plumage and black tail. Two guitars and a box drum made up the trio of musicians. Some of the Latino guests danced flamenco, others kept time to the music with their cutlery. An Australian couple dressed entirely in camouflage fatigues discussed cannibalism in Papua New Guinea, a family of five Argentine doctors drew 'fundoplication' techniques on paper napkins for a forthcoming conference in Arequipa, while a Scandinavian and his girlfriend (or was it his daughter?) huddled on the small balcony hanging over the train track.

Jaime came to sit beside her.

"So, you like this?"

"I do!" she said, eyes shining. "More than 'like.' I feel at home here." And she did. Speaking the language helped, but there was something about the air, the light, the colour and the history fossilised at every turn, that resonated with her.

"Then you should come to Colombia, to Cartagena de Indias." The man's eyes, this stranger's eyes were watchful behind his dark glasses. Dressed in a pristine white guayabera and panama hat like hers, he was the epitome of the Latin American gentleman. With a certain sense of superiority as if recognising something of one in the other, she noted they were the only two well-dressed passengers. They *looked* Spanish.

"Cartagena de Indias …" He touched her wrist lightly. "Will heal …" he made a vague gesture towards her heart. "Whatever pain there is there, whatever is stopping you from being truly happy."

"B-but I am happy!" she protested.

Jaime beckoned to the waiter and ordered two Pisco Sours. "No," he said. "No, you're not."

"There's too much guilt," he said when the waiter returned with tumblers of the celery- coloured traditional drink, frothy with an egg-white topping. "You bend with the wind - relying too much on what others think of you. Be yourself." He glanced at the exquisite detail of her blouse. "You are of course at one level but on another…" his voice trailed.

Carla felt the familiar surge of panic she did when anyone expressed an interest in her. She knew that she could appear confident, outgoing even, that her soignèe appearance created a certain impression. But that was armour to preserve her aloofness. If truth be told, she was afraid that if anyone really got to know her, they'd be disappointed. She took a gulp of her pisco, feeling its potency like a drug, making everything feel a little distended. How did this this stranger dare tell her how she felt? How was a stranger able to read her so accurately?

"*Tranquila,*" he continued. "Go at life gently. There's no urgency. And don't place everything in one person. You have so much to give, but you are you." He finished off in English. It came out as '*Dju* are *dju.*'

Oh, but there is! She wanted to say, *there's an urgency to live every moment at full speed so that the energy deployed in doing so would outrun her, blot out the pain.* He was right, though. In other circumstances or when she was younger, she might have bristled at being mildly lectured, but she was feeling mellow again thanks to the pisco and the lilt of his South American accent.

"You're very ... perceptive," she said pleasantly. "How do you know all this?" He was dressed (and behaved) like a man of leisure, as interested in fashion as she was. He said nothing, finished his drink and leant back on the padded bench against tapestry cushions, the ceiling to floor windows framing his head in jungle greenery.

"We're passing through Wiñay Wayna" he said motioning to steeply terraced stones jutting out from a perch above them. "These beautiful ruins weren't discovered until the 1940s. If you were walking along the Inca trail, you'd be able to visit them."

"And what does it mean, Winy W-?"

Jaime smiled. "It means, my dear, 'Forever Young', in Quechua."

"And have you been?"

"Many, many times. Can't you tell?"

But the leisurely journey was coming to an end. The train chugged through a final verdant valley dotted with grazing llamas before grinding to a halt at Aguascalientes. Making her farewells to Jaime, Carla rushed from the observation carriage back to her seat. Seb was texting on his phone with the blind half down. She reached over him to pull on the toggle. It shot up with a cracking sound. Not only Seb, but a couple of older, dozing passengers jumped.

"Sorry!" she mouthed to no one in particular. "But look!" she said grabbing her handbag. "We're here! We're actually here!"

In her joy at realising a life-long dream (which she assumed was also his), Carla failed to register Seb's annoyance, his coolness, his complete lack of enthusiasm.

The train station was an eye-opener teaming with travellers of all ages and abilities. Carla was astonished to see elderly people who could barely walk, bravely making their way across crowded pavements. Vendors jostled cheek by jowl, selling Machu Pichu replicas, plastic statues of the Sapa Inca Pachacuti, and the same acrylic Peruvian jumpers and scarves that could be found across the whole of South America. There were woven cotton bags in primary colours, jewellery and bin loads of artisan hats - toques with straggly knitted plaits, that to Carla's mind, infantilised grown men.

And still, the women were captivated by so much razzle-dazzle, as they followed snake-like through the covered market, heads darting this way and that, to their waiting bus. There was so much colour and life, food, massages, beauty treatments - everything and anything on offer in the narrow streets. Musicians beat out the tempo with songs to 'Pacha Mama' and invitations to consume two for one piscos. Lines of travellers waiting to board crowded buses wound the length of the main street. And patiently waiting to be discovered by this new round of travellers was the 'old mountain' nestling between two forest-clad Andean peaks.

Except Carla wasn't patient. Comforted (and discomforted) by her talk to Jaime, she'd clung to Seb's arm as their creaky bus negotiated the same hairpin turns as everyone else, but they had been spared having to queue or jostle for a seat. Vertiginous drops on one side were met with over-hanging rocks on the other. Her husband sat impassively, his face shaded by his Akubra. Seb wasn't troubled by altitude provided he was in a vehicle. Helicopters, zip wires left him unfazed and yet he'd found the high ridges of the Atacama Desert problematic, the Great Wall of China went unclimbed. Carla, by contrast, didn't mind heights provided her feet were firmly on the ground. As they lurched around terrifying bends, so did her stomach. And just as she was about to ask the driver to stop, so that she could walk the last bit, the bus ground to an abrupt halt.

"This is it?"

Carla suppressed a pang of disappointment. The pretty watercolour in her Belmond brochure depicted a two-story stone bungalow (only thirty-two rooms) with large windows.

The accompanying literature described it as a small lodge and 'the only hotel at the entrance' to the iconic site. But, now that she thought about it, other photographs, especially the ones that gave the impression of seclusion, were slightly grainy. Carla remembered that last one in particular because it had fanned her romantic nature. A glamorous couple were shown strolling hand in hand (it was an easy leap to imagine herself and Seb) through a garden described as 'an oasis of calm.' To the rear of the lodge, nestling below the steep granite terraces of Machu Pichu were more outdoor spaces where the quiet was disturbed only by the buzz of hummingbirds, the creak of rattan furniture when you reached for another pisco. Carla should have read the blurb more carefully. 'At the entrance' was significant. So was 'small.' In fact, so too was 'oasis'. In reality, the 'lodge' felt more like a Premier Inn back home. It was undoubtedly, 'at the entrance' - at the ticket entrance that is, to Machu Pichu itself. They'd arrived in front of the hotel but so too had *all* the tour buses for the region. Back-packers and exhausted visitors filed in front of them throwing off resentful glances as Carla swept up the short flight of steps to be handed a tepid towel. The place had the feel of a cheap Chinese restaurant in Portsmouth - the kind she'd been to with Sophie.

No matter, thought Carla, surely afternoon tea would be as described. She hankered after silver teapots on white linen, delectable finger food and the tiny sandwiches and feather-light sponge cake served in expensive hotels. She wasn't hungry, but she was gasping for a cup of tea. She smiled thinly, although Seb didn't seem to notice either her disappointment or the place. For which she'd booked two nights. At a grand a night. She did a little gulp. Still, she supposed it beat queuing down in Aguascalientes and the private tour scheduled for that afternoon was included.

Although she was beginning to wonder what 'private' might actually mean. She darted ahead, half hoping to see Jaime and join him, to elegantly position herself at a tiny French-style table.

"O-kaay," said Seb. No sooner had they stepped inside the lodge than they were met with nothing short of a scrum. 'Tea' was self-service with the same people who had been fed champagne and snacks solidly from 9 a.m. that morning: canapés, aperitives and lunch, now grabbing food as if they'd been starved for days. There was no holding back, certainly no manners nor many empty tables. Carla removed her hat, shaking out her hair.

"God!" she said. "This is awful! I'm going to powder my nose."

Suddenly, Seb, who had hardly spoken during the entire train journey roused himself.

"I'll find a table," he said manfully. "You go freshen up, and I'll have your tea waiting. English Breakfast, yes? No, Coca?"

Carla shook her head. "No Coca thanks - not sure it actually does anything."

She squeezed past a family of Ecuadorians who like her, seemed disappointed. They were all dressed in a variation of jogging gear. The overweight father had smartened his with a heavy gold necklace and a cap worn back to front. His wife's pink and purple Spandex looked borrowed from their teenage daughter, while their eldest boy's pants were so low on the hip Carla could see the band of his Calvin Klein underwear. They looked like the cast from *The Sopranos*, but later Carla learned that the mother was the foremost breast cancer oncologist in her country and the boy was a whizz at maths.

"*Increíble*," said the mother.

Carla made a 'totally agree' face.

"And do you know, that apart from today's tour, if you want to re-visit Machu Pichu, you have to book? It's not included. A lot of the sessions for tomorrow are taken already. I just checked. Plus, there's a limit on how long you can be in the 'park.' I guess you're staying tonight and not going back later?"

Carla's eyes widened, uncertainty further flattening her mood. She hated having to worry about bookings. They were supposed to be all nice and relaxed by this stage with the most challenging part of their trip behind them.

"Is that right? Sorry, yes, we're staying. Two nights."

"Then you need to go to the ticket office *pero ya*. Just take whatever time slot is offered; otherwise, you won't be able to see anything. And as we leave first thing in the morning, the day after tomorrow, it's your only chance."

Carla nodded, no longer needing the loo. She hurried back to the dining room where Seb, who had been virtually monosyllabic since the morning, was chatting animatedly to a pretty Peruvian girl dressed entirely in white. Seb, the girl and the girl's partner were squashed in together at the end of a cafeteria-type table.

"*Hola*," said Carla coolly.

Seb jumped to his feet to make the introductions. He had already consumed chocolate cake and coffee.

"It was only small," he said, indicating an inch with his thumb and index finger. The girl found him hilarious.

"I'm sure it was," said Carla finding him less so. "Seb -"

But her husband was into his stride.

"Quite the Renaissance man," said the girl's companion. "Is there anything your husband can't do?"

"I ask myself that all the time."

"I know, I know," agreed Seb.

"I mean," purred the girl. "Polo, marine biology... and now a *painter*? I mean wow! Too much."

"Isn't it?"

Carla glanced away from the girl - she really was very striking with jet black hair and a low-cut top - back to Seb and tried to see him objectively as this girl must, the way she had when they first met. His eyes were an even darker blue, now that his face was tanned. It was a lean, face with a long nose and arched brows. It was still a face that made her heart flip.

"How *do* you keep up?"

Except when idiots like this woman said things like that.

Carla glared.

"She tries," said Seb loving himself.

Carla would have kicked him had she been sitting down.

"Have a seat," said Seb as if reading her thoughts. He made a half-hearted attempt to rise, but he was genuinely hemmed in.

"That's OK," said Carla. "I'll have some tea later."

"Oh, tea!" Seb mockingly touched his forehead. *"Pacha Mama!* I forgot."

Pacha Mama?

The girl looked at him, adoringly. "Spanish too, huh? There has to be *something* wrong with the guy, right?"

Carla ignored her. "It's OK," repeated Carla. "I don't want tea. Seb," she said urgently. "We've got to book for tomorrow. What time ideally? I'm going to do it right now-"

Magic words as it turned out because this time, Seb managed to jump to his feet. And spill coffee all over the Peruvian's very white top and palazzo pants.

Not quite so adorable now, huh?

Carla's sympathetic cooing was soon drowned by the girl's screams as Seb made matters worse by grabbing the corner of the tablecloth, thinking it was a napkin. In a gesture worthy of the nimblest magician, plates and cutlery landed back on the table. Except for the little pots of strawberry jam and *dulce de leche* - that sweet, caramel-coloured conserve popular in Argentina which has a particularly cloying consistency. After the commotion had died down with waiters dashing to the rescue, Carla breathed a sigh of relief. Short-lived as it turned out.

"Great. Come with-" she'd tried to take Seb's hand, but his fingers slid away to her wrist, her waist, any bit of her if fact that he could get hold of, almost lifting her off her feet in his urgency to remove her from the restaurant.

"What's the matter?" Carla made for the entrance the minute

he let go, but Seb pulled her back towards the stairs to their room. Not that she'd seen it yet, but the hotel was small enough that she guessed bedrooms were on the second floor. The ground floor seemed to be taken up entirely by this cafeteria-style restaurant. "The ticket office is outside. We have to-"

"Book for one," interrupted Seb quickly. "I have to go back to England. There's a meeting I just can't get out of. I'm sorry, but I can't stay. You're going to have to book tickets for one."

7

"Evensong's off," said Seb glancing at his phone. He'd zipped up his gilet. He looked better for having had some sun recently. Blue shirts always complimented his swarthy looks, especially when he was tanned. He'd also lost weight and the garment, which was a departure from his usual get-up, made him look put together and youthful.

Carla was still screwing on the back of her earring.

"What do you mean? You mean you aren't coming?"

"No," said Seb patiently. "I mean it's been cancelled."

"Oh," said Carla deflated. She'd been looking forward to seeing her friends while at the same time having some downtime, resting her head against the wooden pew, closing her eyes. Just 'being' as Sophie was continually telling her. *'You don't have to fill every silence with chat.'* Oh, but she did! Silences were loaded, silences were secrets, betrayals about to happen - silences changed one's world from predictable and happy to aching and agonising.

"There's talk of closing churches."

Carla blinked. Events were happening too quickly for her to fully grasp. She felt dizzy with the speed with which old routines were being pulled; no *yanked* from under her.

"But surely not the Cathedral?" It was unthinkable.

"Even the Cathedral."

Carla's phone pinged. She was supposed to be meeting a

group of girls she'd been at school with (they called themselves 'Les Girls') on the weekend. Text messages were coming in fast and furious.

Meant to be organising work event next week but think it might be cancelled

Mum's care home is now closed to all visitors, and I only went to see her this morning!

Carla scrolled down to the arguments for 'social isolating'. What was that anyway? She had every intention of carrying on as usual.

She looked up. "Yes, all right - no Evensong."

Another ping.

Going to be very unpopular and suggest we postpone our London meeting

No! Carla texted back furiously. *Let's not!*

Worry about the vulnerable members of my family ...

One of their group was a doctor, and now she was in on it as well texting:

Great Ormond St. and other places making plans to deal only with intensive care patients - think schools should be closed- the government wants us to get herd immunity -

Couldn't find loo paper or pasta or rice on my weekly shop

Can we wait till midweek before deciding?

Oh, yes, please! Yes, oh, sensible one!

Thank goodness for Gem!

Of course, we must put our health and safety first, but we need to see each other, don't we?

Yes, again, yes!

Carla shoved her phone in her bag. She felt flat without the prospect of seeing people later. Still, she could spend time with Alfie when he woke up. If he ever did. She brushed past Seb.

"I'm going for a swim," she said. "While I still can."

Carla nosed her car up Canon Street, hoping that she wouldn't face any oncoming traffic. Because of its extreme windy narrowness, let alone proximity to schools in the centre of town, the street was usually a tangle of parents trying to edge their way past each other. More often than not, they'd be forced to reverse all the way down again. In addition to this, along with bicycles, scooters and prams, College boys used the road as a shortcut to school from the boarding houses dotted along St. Cross Road and beyond. Today it was disconcertingly empty. The M3 wasn't. In fact, the motorway was as congested as usual - no sign at all that anything untoward was occurring in the country. When she got to her sports' club, it was also busy, and the outdoor pool had its usual smattering of hardened swimmers - women like herself who swam outside all year round no matter the weather.

"Still open then?" she said, commenting the obvious as she swiped her pass.

"Oh, yeah." The girl on the desk beamed. "Staying open till we're told otherwise."

"Glad to hear it."

But in the changing room, the talk was different with speculation as to how long leisure clubs would stay open. Carla alternated from feeling optimistic that reports about this virus were exaggerated, to pessimism that they might not be.

"A matter of days," someone said.

"Swim while you can," said another.

"Schools are closed in Canada until September."

Carla's heart sank. *September? That was insane. That would never happen here. They might close for a few weeks but no longer, surely?*

"It's not possible!"

The women looked at her. She hadn't realised that she'd spoken aloud.

"My lot have left uni," said Kitty one of the swimmers with whom Carla was most friendly. "Oli says that people in hall have realised that the virus will go around like wildfire, so everyone's leaving. His Polish friend is going back on Sunday, but he'll have to isolate for two weeks when he gets home."

"Poland will close border in four hours," interrupted one of the Polish cleaners gloomily. All but Carla ignored her.

"Well, I intend to continue as normal," said Carla snapping apart her rubber cap, stuck together after a month's neglect. She'd have to get a new one. It was speckled with black dots.

"Fine for you if you're not one of the compromised groups," said the wild-haired woman who always parked her kit in the same locker. She had thick hair that curled in tight corkscrews, a youthful physique and an enviably flat stomach. "If you have any underlying health issue or elderly parents then you have to act much more responsibly."

"Yes, I get it," muttered Carla suddenly tired, irritated and fighting an irrational urge to cry.

"I don't think you do." Corkscrew woman kicked her sports bag out of the way while she leaned down to fish out her goggles. "See, that's what happened in Italy where the young carried on as usual because *they're* not in danger. The spread through healthy people has been a disaster - that's why the government has resorted to enforcing isolation by law. So, carry on, but you need to think of those who may suffer as a result."

"You don't want to be a super spreader!"

Not the time to mention just returning from Colombia or the States then ...

Carla was feeling more deflated by the minute.

"At least it doesn't seem to be affecting very young children," she said feebly. There was clearly nothing feeble about this disease. She'd read somewhere that all kind of gunk came out of the lungs. Her mind immediately clouded with visions of *Alien.* "This virus, or whatever it is, could be a lot worse. It could be like the Black Death." She thought of Isaac Newton working from home in the year when the Bubonic Plague reached its height. He'd considered it to be his most productive and during that time had developed theories on calculus, optics and gravity. Les Girls had messaged that - perhaps they would all use the time productively.

"They need to close the schools," Corkscrew lady said dismissing Carla's facile comment and backing away from her, covering her face with a towel.

"Er - not sure about that," chipped in Kitty. "Parents need to keep working in hospitals and *not* look after their children. What they can't do, is have the grandparents look after their kids while they go to work."

"Yes," agreed someone else. "It'll defeat the purpose."

"God, bring back Brexit!" someone called from the far end of the changing room. "I'm beginning to miss it."

Oh, so am I! She'd even welcome #MeToo talk (although that seemed to have waned in the wake of this virus), Laurence Fox (she was a fan) and positively bring on anything woke. Carla muttered the new goodbye - something along the lines of 'Stay Safe' and a wave of an elbow. A short while ago, this might have seemed affected, theatrical even, but now it was mere politeness.

She slipped past the women still discussing the latest government tweets. There was also a fast-growing number of memes and video clips, new to this country, but actively flourishing in others where lockdown had already been enforced for some time. Some were hilarious, and Carla applauded the genius humour behind them. Hundreds had to do with loo rolls. She found those less amusing but she'd loved the one showing a Brazilian guy throwing oil on his kitchen floor and using it as a running machine. But her absolute favourite, concerned a man, who, when offered the option of A) staying home with his wife and children or B) … answers 'B' immediately without waiting to hear what' B' is. It was an industry in itself.

Buoyed by the thought that British stoicism would prevail,

Carla went outside to the pool. She tucked her hair in her tighter than usual cap and adjusted her looser than usual goggles. Normally, she would plunge in straight away, gasping with shock as her body hit icy water, then swim as fast she could to warm up. Instead, she registered the the pool's temperature with disbelief. The water was warmer than it had been in Cartagena. Gingerly, she swam a couple of lengths just to make sure that her body temperature hadn't risen as a result of the virus or some other infection. But no, the pool was still deliciously warm. She felt herself unwind, her muscles relax and her thoughts turn to the week ahead. She'd accepted that there wouldn't be any music at the Cathedral, but there were other events scheduled in the diary to look forward to, including a girls' lunch. Surely, all the hysteria regarding this virus was just that? If all else failed, there was always swimming.

As Carla swam the front crawl, so did her mind - strident strokes, buoyant and flat against the water's surface, her breathing quick and sharp. And all the time, her fluttering feet and palms, pushing hard against her body's movement, took her further away from the Southampton club and closer to the memory of their recent holiday in Cartagena. Cartagena de Indias, delectable Caribbean Cartagena. She flipped onto her back. The sky here, was as insipid as the other was vibrant. She recalled the city's most flamboyant houses painted in pops of yellow and green or pink and orange or then again turquoise and taupe. The pool's chlorinated water was so warm that she was quickly transported to that other intense heat rising from dusty cobblestones. She thought of the street vendors breaking open coconuts with a machete, the Plaza de los Coches with its clock tower that divided the old town from the edgy chaos

of the new. With every muffled sound underwater, she
remembered the clip-clop of horse-drawn carriages, ghosts of
a bygone age and yet still at home in that Colonial seaport
city. Strong African women, swathed in off-the-shoulder
ruffles of red, yellow and blue - colours of the Colombian
flag, balanced vast baskets of fruit on their turbaned heads
while offering to have their photo taken. If you caught their
eye, they sashayed slowly forward, walking clichés - the very
embodiment of seduction - yet no less entrancing, no less
irresistible.

As she slid through the water, her thoughts turned just as
smoothly to her birthday celebrations - champagne and
lobster in the courtyard of the legendary Santa Clara Hotel
with its potted emerald-green ferns, orchids, roses and
tubular flowers. Carla had worn her floaty Valentino dress
(one she'd bought in Sydney on her way to New Zealand the
previous year) and Chanel sandals. Waiters sang 'Happy
Birthday' on three different occasions throughout the day,
and Seb had given her a necklace of semi-precious stones. It
was a perfect birthday. Within the context of now, it was
perfect. Juxtapositioned against what had been, it would
never be enough - nothing could ever erase what had
happened.

Carla approached the end of the lane, executed a neat flip
turn and kept swimming. But her mind wasn't as disciplined.
With every length, other memories slipped under the radar.
All the time, she pretended that the lovely warm water was
the shimmering sea of the Caribbean or any warm water in
fact, other than a chlorinated public pool at Lords Hill. *Agua
caliente* - 'warm water' which was only two letters away from
Aguascalientes. One step further and it became the near
fiasco associated with it. Carla would never forget the
excitement of arriving at the base of Machu Pichu followed

not long after by Seb's shock announcement that he was going back to England.

The rest of their trip was also in jeopardy- the part that promised to be the highlight. They were to travel to Arequipa on the famous Andean Explorer along one of the world's highest railways. The duration of the trip was to be five days, three nights, and would take in Lake Titicaca on the way. The wardrobe for that leg of the journey had given Carla sleepless nights, cost thousands of pounds and taken months to assemble. Not to mention the *actual* train fare - she could have bought a small flat with what that had cost. Or a car. Certainly, a Hermès handbag. Either way, it was no understatement to say it was to be the trip of a lifetime. And now Seb was saying he had to fly back to England (to a meeting he must have known about), and that he couldn't accompany her any further. The ringing in her head was deafening. His voice had faded. The only thing she understood was that he couldn't go.

"But *you* can," he'd said as red-eyed, she'd finally come out of the bathroom.

"Not alone!" she'd snarled.

"Well, I'm sure you won't be for long," he'd retorted not unkindly. "There's always that Jaime character."

"Wh- *Jaime?* Are you kidding? I don't want to be with a stranger! I want to go with you! We've planned it - I've been looking forward to it. You know I have."

It felt as though (again) her world had crashed. It was these trips that kept her going; kept her marriage going, not to put too fine a point on it.

"I'm sorry," said Seb looking admittedly more remorseful even then when that other thing had happened. "I truly am. But I have to be there. The company is meeting. People are coming from Australia."

"They're meeting in *Milton Keynes*," she'd spat. "Not London or New York!"

"Yes, but Richard's coming from Oz."

"Only because he was going to be over anyway, not *especially*. You can *skype* for God's sake. People do it all the time. You said so yourself, that you could *be* anywhere."

"Except this time. I'm needed."

"*I* need you. Don't do this, Seb. Don't!"

"I'm sorry."

"That's all you can say?" She was hiccupping now. "I'll never ever forgive you."

He ran his hand through his long hair - she was momentarily distracted by the thought that it didn't have a streak of grey.

"But you will," he said.

"I won't," She hadn't over the other. Not that Seb would ever know; she pretended pretty well. "Fuck you."

She'd gone back into the bathroom, her laptop tucked under her arm, slamming the door hard and locking it. She was shaking, her voice had risen, and she was sure the entire Sanctuary Lodge could hear them. She didn't care. She looked at herself in the mirror; the vein pulsating down the middle of her forehead. This couldn't be happening. Except, how many times had she'd said that before? Her sobs gradually subsided, then blinding anger gave way to practicality. She sat on the edge of the bath. She *could* go by herself, as Seb suggested. She'd envisioned them both travelling through the snow-covered La Raya mountains pisco in hand. She thought of the beautiful en-suite cabin she'd booked - there were only two on the forty-eight-guest, seventeen-carriage train, along with the requisite observation car and dining wagons. The cabins looked luxurious: polished timber, linen-covered walls, chairs strewn with textiles in Peruvian motifs and soft baby alpaca throws. Even the basins looked beautiful carved in local stone. *This* one certainly wasn't - something you'd expect to find in a Travel Lodge. She began removing mascara with a cotton bud. She'd spent most of her first marriage alone in an empty bed. She wasn't going to be that sad woman on her own. She cleaned her teeth, splashed her face with water.

Right. Well, if Seb wasn't coming with her, Carla would cancel the whole damn thing. She could imagine her friends asking her how it had all gone and her response: *'We loved Machu Pichu - but guess what? We had to cancel the next bit - I know - I know. But what can you do? Seb had a meeting - yeah, it's his baby - he feels so responsible. Always. God, I know! Never mind we'll go next year.' 'Not sooner?' 'No, the weather in the Andes etc. etc. so...'* and then the gasps of disbelief followed by a rush of support because *'there is always something in the unhappiness of others that does not displease us ...'*

Only her pride was getting in the way now. There *was* an alternative. She could, of course, be loyal and supportive - in short, the perfect wife. And she just might have been, had the other not happened. And that was the problem, wasn't it? The problem with forgiveness. An easy thing to grant at the time but *with* time, just when you thought you'd moved on, the resentment came back stronger than before. How long had it been anyway? Ten years? A whole decade had not dulled the memory. Carla felt calmer. Somehow, it helped understanding that her brittle reaction to things was due to the other. And because of the other, everything was fragile between them. It took so little for raw emotion to scratch through to the surface - to tear at the healing scab and make it bleed. Nah, she wasn't that wife. Not anymore.

Carla logged onto the British Airways site changing her ticket for the day after. Fuck it - if she had to return, she'd go 'First'. *All* the way. No 'Business' for certain legs of the journey home. Taking into account the different time zones, it wasn't going to be a direct trip. She'd have to make her way back to Cusco and then to Lima again, when they'd been originally due to fly out of Buenos Aires. She booked a taxi to meet her at Heathrow, watching the pounds exiting from her online account. But she didn't cancel their train tickets - only Perurail could amend those. She'd get reception to ring the company on her behalf in the morning. She was exhausted - so tired that despite the upset, she thought she might just sleep.

She came out of the bathroom.

"All done. For me, that is."

Seb nodded.

"Yeah, I'm going back cattle."

That's too bad ...

"I can't pay for you now but-"

"Don't worry about it - I've taken care of my ticket."

Seb made a helpless gesture.

"I'll make it up to you - I promise."

Carla looked at him in wide-eyed astonishment.

"How on earth, could you do that?"

"No, you're right," he said quietly.

He looked genuinely distressed, and she could see that he was caught between a rock and a hard place, between what his partner Richard required of him and what she did. However, Seb's inability to confront anything until it quite literally smacked him in the face, infuriated her. If he'd paid for this - let alone *any* of their holidays - she was pretty sure it would be a different story. He'd certainly try harder to think of one to tell Richard.

Carla undressed, lobbing her clothes onto the chair and got into bed. She began crying quietly. It was all too much. *Tell him I'll forgive him if* ... Sophie's words taunted her just when she wanted to think clearly. As if things weren't complicated enough! That was the problem, Carla could never deal *cleanly* with the separate issues that arose between her and Seb - issues that had nothing to do with Sophie - because that other always came back to colour everything. And that was it, wasn't it? It was all to do with Sophie. Even this, now, her reaction exaggerated or not, had to do with Sophie.

God! Carla was so tired of it all. Perhaps it was time to stop going around in circles and decide once and for all, to either forgive and move on, or not. (It was the 'not' that was terrifying). What did have to stop, was this self-destructive cycle. She was no heroine for forgiving Seb. On the contrary, most people would judge *her* (Sophie certainly did). It was ironic; she'd done nothing wrong and yet Carla was the one paying the price, while Seb was forgiven, beloved, popular. He put a hand on her shoulder.

"Carla I -"

"Don't," she said viciously. "Don't! Don't say another word, don't touch me!"

Her body was rigid, aching with the effort of keeping to her side of the bed, without touching any part of him. And there it was; their relationship laid bare - blown apart - a minefield always so close to the surface.

8

As she was leaving the sports' club a few days later, Sophie texted. She was home from the hospital, self-isolating with Ed and wanted vegan yoghurt (any flavour) and liquid paracetamol. Ed said the queues at their local Sainsbury's were too long (he was still at work) so he'd not be able to get to Sophie and back again during his lunch break. Their local pharmacy had also run out of aspirin. *Just leaving now* Carla texted. *Just need to get home, and park, shop and then will come to you* - that is, she wanted to say, when I've turned around and gone virtually back to where I started. There was also a text from Les Girls who had adopted the politicians' lexicon in likening the virus to a wartime enemy. They had new information. It could live on surfaces: glass (four days), paper (four to five days), plastic (five days,) aluminium (two to eight hours), surgical gloves (eight hours), steel (forty-eight hours) and wood (four days).

Carla accelerated along the now empty motorway suspecting that she'd just had her last swim and that the David Lloyd (following the example of countless other clubs and leisure centres around the country) would be closing imminently. On the other hand, it wasn't as if she had anything else to do. Alfie was still asleep - he was *always* sleeping when she left the house - and Seb was working. Life for Seb was continuing pretty much the same as usual, albeit without the lovely fun, frothy bits she was used to organising: dinner parties, opera and of course, travel. They had always travelled a great deal and that had only increased when Alfie began boarding.

Carla parked and went into town at her usual pace, stopping to buy a takeaway coffee from Café Monde - always her favourite - where the mood was gloomy. The owner had closed the upstairs seating area. In an attempt to sell off what remained of his confectionary, cakes were displayed in the window, but these had a forlorn look, sagging beneath gloopy dollops of icing.

"You're open!" she said gleefully.

"Yeah, but who knows for how long?"

Not very, as it turned out. By the end of the day, all but essential food stores had closed. Carla regretted not collecting her dry-cleaning. Through the window of the store, she spotted her neatly pressed white linen trousers. "You can hang them outside!" she mouthed to the owner who was sitting behind the counter wearing a mask and gloves. "I'll step away." He shook his head, shooing her away with his hands as though somehow, she might infect him through the pane. "You'll have to wait for three weeks like everyone else!"

From there, she joined the queue snaking around the building at Marks and Spencer. Only four people were being allowed in at one time, but she didn't have long to wait. Shoppers nipped in and out, frightened to be out at all. She spied an acquaintance of hers, a fit young woman who worked in a clothes shop Carla sometimes frequented. The woman wore a mask and gloves and was too jittery to talk. "You're not scared, are you?" Carla asked in disbelief. "To death!" the woman replied jigging on the spot." And if you had the sense that God gave you, you'd be too!"

A group call from Les Girls - the doctor among them had just had lunch with her daughter in a deserted restaurant in

London - kept her distracted. One of the group's son was on his way home from India as treks and beauty spots had closed. Someone else's brother had come out of retirement to volunteer at his local hospital. Yet another's daughter had been in tears when her school cancelled her A-levels. "*Tears?*" Carla echoed. "Can you imagine if *our* O-levels had been cancelled?"

"You're up," said a gloved M&S assistant.

"Got to go," said Carla ringing off. But once in the shop, keeping her distance was easy. Anyone she came face to face with, scurried away in fear. Carla felt awkward hovering at any one counter, as though choice itself had become an indulgence. She also struggled to find the non-dairy yoghurt Sophie could digest. Shopping was no longer a casual exercise and when she reached the chemist, people were queuing the length of the market square. A security guard emerged as she arrived, to announce that Boots had run out of both aspirin and paracetamol.

"Wash your hands!" barked Seb when she got home and had dumped her shopping just inside the door. "Wash your hands!" There was a rising note of hysteria in his voice as he rushed to meet her. He hovered, making sure that she didn't touch anything on her way to the bathroom before going into the kitchen.

"You have to understand," he said as though talking to a child. "The virus isn't a living organism, but a protein covered by a layer of fat. When absorbed by cells in your eyes and nose, it mutates into something aggressive. And it's fragile, so that's why any soap is the best remedy. The soap cuts the fat."

"Thank you for explaining," said Carla. She wasn't being

sarcastic. She was too preoccupied to even try.

"I'd hug you," added Seb, apologetically. "But you might be infected."

Carla shrugged, ignoring this. "I have to go out again anyway," she said. "I still need to get aspirin. Boots has run out."

Seb didn't hesitate to offer some of the stash she knew he had.

"That's kind, but it has to be in liquid form," she said warmed by his response. "Sophie can't swallow properly. She's waiting for an op, but I guess that won't happen until this Corona thing is over."

"I'll go," said Seb grabbing his wallet from the hall table. "I'll get you some. They know me. Won't be long."

"Hope not," said Carla thinking of the Eastern Block feel of queuing for food. Although of course, here, there was still food to be had. She remembered being in St. Petersburg in the '80s when there was neither choice nor fresh food. "Oh, and if we want bread," she called as he slammed the front door. "We'll have to set the alarm. Hoxton's opens at 8 a.m. but only on a Wednesday!"

Carla's phone pinged. The update from Les Girls was that the virus could spread via petrol pumps. It was advisable to use gloves or paper towels and then dispose of them straight away. Carla ignored that one - it didn't look like they could drive anywhere far even had they wanted to. There was more about downloading a free App called Houseparty and another called Zoom. Carla had heard of neither.

A silence fell when she'd put away her phone. For a moment she stood listening for sounds of life. Upstairs, it was even quieter - suspiciously quiet. She tiptoed up to Alfie's 'lair' - his ship-like accommodation in the attic. The bedroom and bathroom were tiny, but his playroom area was spacious, ideal for entertaining friends. In normal circumstances. Still in his dressing-gown, Alfie was sprawled on a beanbag, playing computer games.

"Hi Mum," said Alfie, stretching out a bare leg in her direction. His feet were only a size off hers. How had he grown so big? "What's for lunch?"

She crouched on the top step.

"Um ... not sure. Have you even had breakfast? I have to go out shortly to see Sophie, but there's sausages and mash. Might have to wait till I get back."

Alfie nodded, the sound of gunfire in the background.

"What are you playing?" she asked apprehensively. "Not Fortnite, I hope."

Alfie blew her a kiss. "Of course not!" he said with a winsome smile. "*Non, non, non,*" he added with a mock French accent.

The trouble with her youngest was that he could always get around her. Carla took a step into the room, her gaze flickering past the unpacked crate of Lego he'd insisted they bring from the old house. From the dormer window there was a clear view of their former house and garden. She'd never noticed before, how higgledy piggledy the houses all were: some tall and narrow and unadulterated, some squat with modern extensions. Their sloping rooves were on different levels and of varying dimensions. Through a gap in the city wall, she glimpsed geometric corners of the

Cathedral. The flag above the clock tower unfurled into the clouds.

"It's great, isn't it?"

"What is?" Surely, he wasn't enjoying *not* seeing his friends? Not being at school she understood, but she knew he was disappointed not to be playing any cricket or tennis, or being able to visit any of his mates who lived nearby.

"Common Entrance is off - Winchester too."

"*What?*"

Carla whipped out her phone.

"Mum, you don't have to do that!" said Alfie as Carla jabbed the screen. She was nowhere near as tech-savvy as her son.

"I get there in the end," she said desperately searching for the WhatsApp group for his year. "If not as directly as you would. How do you know? About the exams?"

He looked up briefly. "Everyone knows," he said. "We've all been talking about it."

The firing sounds from her son's game, together with the irritating voice-over, with all the disjointedness of an air traffic controller, began ricocheting in her head. So many unknowns rose like the NCP pop-ups in one of Alfie's games - unseen, unknown but decidedly threatening.

And there it was, the message she'd missed earlier. The senior school to which her son was enrolled in the autumn, had decided to wave its entrance exams - measures were being taken to factor in distance learning not only for the next term, but for September as well. *September!* The thought that Alfie could be home for six weeks was bad enough, but six *months!* Carla simply couldn't assimilate the information. She felt giddy. It actually felt that any moment now, a voice would infiltrate their homes to announce the domination of the planet by aliens. Well, the virus *was* an alien of some description. No longer a 'beeruus' to joke about, this was a deadly virus destroying their way of life.

"Have to drop off some groceries for Sophie," she said weakly.

"Love ya, Mum," said Alfie cheerfully.

"Love you too," said Carla less so.

"Hello, the house!" she heard Seb call, arriving home. Carla dashed to the stairs, pushing Alfie's hair out of his eyes as she flew past him. He immediately shook it back into place. "And get dressed!" she threw over her shoulder.

Seb stood in the hall, a big grin on his face, his gilet bulging.

"Ta da!" he announced with a flourish, for a moment forgetting his strict policy on hand washing the minute they came into the house. "Liquid paracetamol. Prescription even."

Carla was genuinely astonished. "How on *earth* did you manage it?" But her spirits soared. What a result! She couldn't wait to tell Sophie!

Seb looked equally pleased. His eyes danced.

"The girl on the prescriptions' counter knows me. *Technically*, they've sold out of paracetamol, but they always hold some back. I told her about Sophie - how she's just come out of the hospital."

Carla took a step towards him.

"Uh, uh." He shook his head. "Have to wash first."

"Yeah," she said. "I forgot. We can't touch."

"You always touch me," he said softly. For a moment, he held her gaze. "You probably *should* leave the package 30 minutes though," he added gruffly. "To be on the safe side."

"That's fine," said Carla scooping up the medicine and dropping it in her handbag. "I'll take the risk. Besides, Sophie's waiting for her lunch." She gestured to the yoghurt she'd left on the entrance table. "She's been waiting a while."

Seb nodded. "Well, be careful. Don't get too close."

Carla was silent. *I'll get as close as I want. I will never be kept away again ...*

Except that she was. Knocking on Sophie's door an hour later and standing a respectful distance, Ed came to the door, dishevelled and barefoot - not exactly rushing to greet her. Warily, they eyed each other up. Despite Ed being a long-term boyfriend, Carla had only met him recently, shortly before Sophie's latest bout of illness. She could only guess at what her daughter had told him - all of it correct of course, except for the forgiveness part, the *'Tell him I'll forgive him if...'* That last was crucial for Carla. It explained at least to herself, why she had taken Seb back. It was the cue that allowed Carla *to* take him back. But Carla also knew that no matter *what* she did to show Sophie how much she loved her, it didn't make any difference. But that didn't mean Carla would give up trying, that the hurt ever diminished.

"I've brought the yoghurt, the food S-Sophie wanted," she stammered, suddenly uncertain. £50 worth of yoghurt to be precise. Carla had bought every flavour she could find of the non-dairy variety and a basket of hyacinths. Sophie loved all shades of the colour blue. "And -" this was her trump card - "the paracetamol!"

Ed's frostiness melted, and a kindly smile broke over his face. Carla had liked him when she first met him, and she liked him even more now. It was clear that he cared a great deal about Sophie. "Oh, that's great!" he said, opening the door a little wider. "Thank you. You know, I'm sorry about the other day," he added. "I was just following orders."

"Oh, don't worry about that," said Carla breezily. "I understand completely. Sophie can be a little stern."

"You can say that again!"

They smiled conspiratorially, Carla suppressing a hysterical giggle. Her hands were shaking as she set down the shopping. She knew better than to hand it to him directly.

"What can I be?" said Sophie coming up behind Ed. She was tiny in comparison and having been ill, seemed waif-like and frail. Her hair - typically ash blonde - was lank, and there were huge circles under her eyes. She appraised her mother coldly.

"Oh, darling!" said Carla taking a step towards her, longing to hold her in her arms.

Sophie hid behind Ed.

"You need to stay away." Her head poked through the crook of Ed's arm. Her expression softened as Carla stepped back so that she was standing in the middle of the road. No danger of passing traffic; the place was deserted.

"I've brought you what you wanted," said Carla limply.

"Yeah, thanks." Sophie glanced down at the shopping bags poking one with her toe.

"Er ... Not sure that I can eat yoghurt."

But that's what you wanted this morning!

"Oh. Oh, well, no problem." £50 down the drain ...

"Yeah," continued Sophie, chewing the end of her hair, the way she used to when she was little. "Dad was here. Really amazing! He brought me a tray of Sushi all the way down from London. He got some restaurant to prepare it for me. He's the best."

London! Then Carla fervently hoped the fish had been packed in a lot of ice. Her outer shell wanted to yelp like a dog that had been kicked out of the way. That's exactly what she was, a fawning dog coming back for more. She settled for a hollow, "Yes, isn't he?"

Ed muttered something about not being able to ask her in. At least he had the grace to look embarrassed. "Take care of ..." Carla was about to say 'yourself', but Sophie had already vanished, so she ended up addressing the 'her' to Ed. "Stay safe," she said, kicking herself for sounding so cringey.

By the time Carla got home, Les Girls had pinged with the latest thought for the day. With uncanny foresight, Bill Gates had given a talk a few years before, anticipating the impact a pandemic might have on humanity. Carla scanned the page. Its selfless message was all about the disease being a great leveller, a reminder that humankind was equal regardless of culture, creed and race, that our health was precious, that we purchased unnecessary goods (Carla's conscience was pricked at the thought of the new Dior tweed jumpsuit she'd just purchased online), and most of all, it was a reminder of how important family was. Gates had ended by saying that a pandemic would force 'us back into our houses so we can rebuild them into our own home and strengthen our family unit.'

Carla, forced back into the quiet of hers, went straight up to their bedroom. Alfie was still upstairs if the rat-a-tat of gunfire was anything to go by, and Seb had gone for a walk. Their new bed was the most comfortable they'd ever owned, and now the gloomy news and the damp bone-setting cold drove her to dive under the covers fully dressed. She'd never been a big sleeper and napping was not something she ever did - not even when she'd had the children. Especially then. Her maternity nurse had forced Carla to sit quietly of an afternoon - or at least Alfie's had - the other one had set her out every day on pointless and draining tasks (like buying starch for baby's bibs) so that she could watch Wimbledon in peace with 'her baby' while she, Carla, wandered the streets lactating messily and fantasising about killing the woman. Which led Carla to ponder the reason why she had allowed herself to be controlled like that. She really was quite pathetic. Even now, Carla was so terrified of her own daughter; she could never be herself. Or just 'be' as Sophie was constantly telling her. *Just be...*

"Ho ho," said Seb what seemed like moments later whipping off his jeans in a flash and sliding under the covers beside her.

Carla's entire body tensed. Grumpily, she moved over to her side of the bed. During that brief hour's sleep, she'd stretched out starfish fashion, luxuriating in having the entire space to herself. Seb's body was burning, all-consuming and her toes sought the coolness of the fresh sheets. He rubbed his head against the new linen bedhead - he liked the feel of it chafing. There was a numb patch on his crown where he'd once been hit by a polo mallet, and sometimes rubbing helped. Automatically, Carla plumped up the pillow behind him. She didn't want the new fabric sporting its own bald patch. His hand came to rest on her thigh. She knew exactly where his thoughts were leading, but these days she fantasised much less about Brad Pitt or Matt Damon (there was a hilarious new meme involving those two) and much more about shops reopening in Stockbridge.

Afterwards, Seb stretched.

"Welcome to lockdown," he grinned. "I guess that's it - everything has closed, no schools, restaurants even the Cathedral."

"But not for Easter?"

"Yup, for Easter."

Incredulous, Carla sank back against the pillows. She appreciated that Evensong had been postponed, but surely by Easter, which was only in a few weeks' time, everything would be back to normal? More importantly, she had ordered a sweet little dress from Milan which she planned to wear on Easter Sunday.

"That's ridiculous. The Cathedral is so enormous, people social distance there as it is. I mean you have to walk to the end of a pew to offer a sign of peace and half the time you're ignored anyway."

"Well, there'll be no more of that. Everything's going to

change," said Seb getting up and dressing, doing up his belt. He could be in and out of his clothes faster than anyone she'd ever met. If only Alfie would take a leaf out of that book. "I've been meaning to ask you. What's your thinking on wearing masks?" He shoved his phone in his pocket, scooping up loose change from the bedside table. For a moment he hovered under the Ramsay print of an 18th Century Chinese mandarin. The pretty watercolour depicting a tea garden and pagoda seemed ironic given that there was now no more infamous place in the world than Wuhan, or that you couldn't name China without evoking a shiver in response.

"No," said Carla sitting up and reaching for her blouse.

"Well, do you think we should take this down?" He flicked the Chinese mandarin a quizzical look. She followed his gaze. The picture looked perfect against the Farrow and Ball 'Zen' palate and the bamboo trim of the frame. She thought of the biography of Lord Snowden she had read recently, and how Princess Margaret had boiled an egg and when it was just the right shade, she'd handed it to her husband who had run with it to a paint manufacturer. Carla would never again think of the colour 'eggshell' in the same light.

"No to that too. And I still think this is all becoming utterly ridiculous. It's stupid."

"Maybe," said Seb patiently, "but it's vital we shut places where large numbers gather."

We? Seb clearly saw himself as one of those analytical, clear-thinking scientists who joined the Chief Medical Officer for daily 5 p.m. updates. Carla thought them panicked and anything but.

"It's *all* about viral loading," he was saying now, "the amount of virus in your blood at first infection, directly relates to the severity of the illness you will suffer later. If you're in a pub say, or religious building or entertainment venue with 200 people, and a large number of people *don't* have symptoms but are shedding, you are breathing in lots of droplets per minute and absorbing a high load of the virus in a crowded space. You'll become ill over 48 hours. If you sit in a room with one person and catch the virus, you get a small viral load. Your immune system will start to fight it, and by the time the virus starts replicating, you'll be ready to kill it."

"But if I sit in the same room with six people all shedding," said Carla. "I get six times the initial dose, and the rise in viral load is faster than my immune system can cope with. So, a family of six people may produce double the droplets of a family of three, in the same space."

"Precisely. But it's also the 'r' number that's becoming crucial, the basic reproduction number - or the average number of people one person with the infection will be likely to infect -"

"So, don't all sit together coughing, is the moral of that story," interrupted Carla.

"You could put it like that." He looked vaguely hurt.

Sex had made Seb mellow; Carla felt frustrated - angry that her world was topsy-turvy, that Alfie was at home, that she couldn't swim, that her plans were being thwarted at every turn. That, if she were really honest, she didn't have enough to do.

"I'm sorry," said Carla contritely. Sometimes, it felt as though his voice was a tiny hammer - the up and down movement of the strings of a piano - blocks halting the smooth progression of her own thoughts. Such as they were. "Go on, I'm listening really," she said to show willing, though unwilling to get out of bed, go downstairs and cook supper.

"It's OK," he said. "But I've got a few ideas about making masks if you want to hear."

Not really. But she didn't say that. She reached for her phone when it pinged, and Seb muttered something about food.

Les Girls again.

Remember to clap for the NHS (emoji of hands) We're doing it at the start of our (Zoom) Pilates class.

Someone else had taken up tapestry; another was baking soda bread for the first time. *No, you don't need yeast, that's the beauty of it!* Carla's head spun with the list of activities on offer via Zoom. She could learn to gut a fish, sing, play poker. *Wouldn't that be great?* There was literally, nothing you couldn't do, except of course, for the one thing that everyone did want, which was to actually see people. National theatres, galleries and opera houses were all (virtually) opening their doors while it seemed that every artist in the world was leaping on to a balcony to belt out some aria or other.

The doctor in the group texted: *Guess what? The malaria drug they're using has retinol toxicity, so my workload will increase.*

And there was something else about Coronavirus deaths being fewer in countries that mandate TB vaccine.

Did you have the BCG inoculation at school?

Carla couldn't remember. Had she?

It was given to every 10-14-year old between 1953 and 2005. At the age of 12 or 13, you had to request it - it was for people who came from or lived in, countries endemic with TB, like India, the Middle and Far East.

Never mind Carla, had her children? She honestly couldn't remember. She glanced at the rest of the chain.

You'd often have a BCG mark on your arm.

Carla took off her blouse to have a look. And left it off. There was so much information to collate, so much *choice*. She closed her eyes again and hoped that this time, she would sleep.

9

Les Girls texted a few weeks later with a funny image of three policemen: a very gorgeous Spanish hunk in a green beret (which matched the colour of his eyes), an equally fit Italian wearing aviator shades and a gun slung low over slim hips and an obese Englishman sitting on a park bench stuffing his face with a doughnut. The only visible weapon in *his* hand was a cup of coffee. Lockdown in Italy and Spain certainly looked easier on the eye than in the UK.

Only momentarily distracted, Carla's head resumed its general fuzziness. She was having trouble sleeping. She would fall into bed exhausted only to wake a couple of hours later, feeling as though there was a clamp on her head - a weight of concrete bricks pushing her back down. If she did dream, her dreams were alarming, vibrant, and she woke up anxious, her heart beating frantically. Sometimes, she imagined she had actually contracted the virus, her head ached so, at other times, her general malaise sent her googling symptoms for MS. The days sloshed backwards and forwards with no purpose, no rhythm to the endless boredom. They had no routine. What was the point? Alfie slept until lunchtime - itself a moveable feast - never changing out of the dressing gown he also slept in. Amazingly, it hadn't begun to smell. Feebly, she asked him to get dressed, and when he refused, she kept silent. What could she say when she wasn't getting dressed either? She wondered now, for whom she'd actually dressed in the past. Besides, it meant that the need to do laundry was virtually non-existent.

What also alarmed Carla about herself during this time, was

the little interest she took in her home. Once, not so very long ago, she had loved nothing better than to shop for this or that decorative object, and then to return home with it and re-arrange her furniture or tweak soft furnishings. She loved sweet-scented interiors; being surrounded by her books and flowers and photographs. Especially those. There were dozens of framed pictures throughout the house, chronicling her life to date. The pictures of the twins were bittersweet - the backstory inevitably involving some drunken episode or other. By contrast, those of Alfie and Seb were joyful and taken against a backdrop of an exotic location.

Exotic locations ... each one seemed as out of reach now, as a trip to the moon. She rifled through her memory, shuffling localities as she remembered them. The earliest photos of Alfie were taken at Guards' Polo Club when he was weeks old. Carla, accompanied by her maternity nurse, had gone to watch Seb play in a tournament. There was a smiling round-faced baby propped up on pillows at the 55 in St. Tropez, there was the toddler sitting on pink sands in Mexico. There were action snapshots taken skiing in St. Moritz, sailing in Fiji, climbing in New Zealand, climbing at Cape Agulhas to see where two oceans meet, or where two rivers collide, in Brazil. Ordinarily, Carla loved being surrounded by and took great comfort in, these glossy reminders of a world made smaller by their travels. Now, they filled her with dread - image after image, a reminder that those wonderful moments were frozen in a past that was growing ever more distant, that so too was her youth. Having Alfie later in life, for a while, had stalled time in her, but now that he too was growing up, Carla felt old, and in a world, she didn't and had no wish to understand.

Really, the only thing that was keeping them going was good food. Seb shopped at M&S for all essential groceries when once they'd only ever have considered Aldi in terms of value for money. They were eating far too much or at least without proper exercise they were, and Alfie who'd always been a skinny little mite was almost her height now and had developed a pot belly. Despite national warnings to go easy, the hoarding of essentials: eggs, porridge and toilet paper, was continuing on epic levels. The Brits continued to be the butt of scatological jokes. They (or rather Seb) spent his life at the shops. Easter came and went, unmarked, and Carla couldn't have cared less. The sweet decorations in the window of the Cornflowers were packed away - not even eggs decorated with little masks made her smile. 31,887 people had now died from Covid - a week earlier the number had been 28,131. Excess deaths above the average, as Seb pointed out, were 50,745.

Carla wasn't sure when her slide into this current lethargy (she baulked at calling it a depression) had begun. Or rather, she did. Exactly when. It had started the last time she'd seen Sophie. There'd been other disappointments and hurts in her life, but somehow that last visit was the proverbial straw. Was it possible to die slowly, over time, of a broken heart? Carla believed it was. She knew that she wasn't behaving maturely or prudently and had attended enough support groups to realise that she'd fallen straight back into old habits of self-pity and reproach. *Bring it on!* She couldn't summon an ounce of energy to combat the despair she was feeling. Nor did she have any wish to. She rather enjoyed just 'being' as Sophie would have called it, although she was pretty sure this wasn't what her daughter had in mind. Sophie was always telling her that 'acceptance' rather than 'resistance' was the way to achieve peace of mind. Well, that's what she was doing. She wasn't resisting at all. For the first time in her entire life, Carla wasn't competing with anyone either professionally, socially or even aesthetically.

Carla marvelled, not just at how quickly the world had ground to a halt, but how fast her own had unravelled alongside in the process. Carla was also amazed that all the things that she'd once cared about no longer seemed to matter, how it had taken this virus to lift the lid off everything. It was undoubtedly true, that without the distractions of ordinary life, the underlying issues of her painful past were now in sharp relief. And with no end in sight to this enforced isolation, she tortured herself with every facet of her relationship with her daughter - yearning for the time again when she could make it all better.

Carla found it most natural to blame Angus and then Seb for everything that had happened to her, but the reality (when she was feeling candid enough to admit it) was that she alone was responsible for the path her life had taken. After that conversation with Jaime on the journey to Machu Pichu, a stranger she was unlikely ever to see again, she had realised something else. It wasn't that she was apprehensive of people getting to know her, it was that she didn't want to know herself. With nothing to look forward to, with nowhere to go, Carla sought amnesia in sleep. She no longer had any idea of what day of the week it was, let alone the hour or month. Les Girls bandied a new lexicon - some of them were being furloughed - so was she Carla decided - to her bed.

"Boris is in intensive care," said Seb coming into their bedroom one day. By Boris, she assumed he meant the prime minister and not their neighbour's dog. She wasn't a fan of either, but she didn't wish them ill. Seb pulled up the blind so that it flapped noisily against the window. Carla winced at the noise, hiding her face in the pillow. "And there's something else," he said quietly. "Ben died last night." They only knew one Ben. Ben who ran the local corner shop - the KPO - Ben who had only recently become close, or close at least, to Seb. Carla had known Ben since she first moved to Hampshire with Angus some thirty years ago. He was more than just a shop manager, he was a good judge of character, able to gauge whether or not a customer was in the mood for a chat. He was someone to whom, at some time or other, everyone revealed secrets, inner anxieties and joys. He was the steady maypole around whom the 'village' that comprised their few streets, danced; whether in sickness or in health. In sickness as it turned out.

"What are you talking about?" said Carla shaken enough out of her lassitude to prop herself up on one elbow. She pushed her sticky, tangled hair out of her eyes. With hairdressers closed, Carla, hadn't been able to get it coloured. To begin with, she'd made do with mascara and whatever WOW colour products she could get her hands on. But even that was a while ago. The odd occasion when she caught sight of herself in the mirror, she saw Indira Gandhi peering back at her.

"But you spoke to him just the other day!" It *felt* like a week ago.

"The day before yesterday. Yes, I know." Seb's eyes were moist. "What I didn't know, was that he had an underlying health condition."

"See," said Carla pouncing. "Just what I've been telling you! It wasn't *Covid* per se."

"He's dead," said Seb his voice ragged with emotion. "He wouldn't be, if it *weren't* for Covid. Plus, he probably didn't want to trouble his doctor."

Carla opened her mouth to contradict him and then shut it. She remembered something her Spanish grandmother had once said to her, about knowing when to stay silent at the very moment it was most tempting to speak. Unfortunately, Carla tended to remember this adage only after the event.

"No," she said. "Of course. You're right." There was a lump in her own throat. Ben. It wasn't possible! Everything around them was changing, but the corner shop didn't. It couldn't, it mustn't. It had.

Seb flung Carla's dressing gown across the bed.

"And for God's sake, get up!"

Carla blinked. "Why?" she said. "Are we going somewhere?"

Seb thrust his hands in his pockets. He was frowning, but even so she felt an unexpected lurch of desire. But she was so miserable over Sophie, that she wouldn't allow herself escapism of any kind. Had things been different she might be enjoying lockdown. She might be doing distance Pilates classes and teaching Alfie to cook scrambled eggs on homemade bread. Grey roots? No problem. She could have dyed her hair with coffee and beetroot juice while running up a little-house-on-the prairie-style frock sewn from discarded curtains à la Sound of Music. She might even have turned to writing self-help guides on how to survive this crisis.

But she wasn't doing any of those things. She wanted to sob at the unfairness of it all, at the loss of Ben. Like a child, she wanted to rail at the gods, shout and scream. She knew she was in denial. She just couldn't accept that any of this madness had become her reality. She didn't want to accept that it had. She didn't want to adapt. And as far as she could see, she didn't have to. Not everyone was thriving during this time. She knew they weren't, from all the funny WhatsApps coming her way. Well, she was a member of *that* club and it was perfectly fine by her.

"We are. All three of us. We're going for a walk."

"B-ut the shops are closed," she said, struggling to process the information. "There's nowhere to go."

"That's right," said Seb patiently. "They are. But we're not going shopping - at least not directly. Had you never considered walking for pleasure?"

"Don't be funny." Carla huddled under the covers. He'd held her attention briefly, but what he was saying was ridiculous. "When on earth was walking ever pleasure? I've never walked anywhere in my life!"

"I know. All the more reason to start now. He whipped away the duvet so that Carla squealed. "You have 30 minutes. I'll deal with Alfie."

An hour and a half later, Carla and Alfie stumbled behind Seb as he marched them down College Street towards the water meadows. It had taken Alfie less than five minutes to get ready. Having never really undressed in the first place, all he'd had to do was clean his teeth and put on his shoes. The shoes were a concession - he'd gone barefoot for two whole weeks. Carla had no idea what he'd been up to in the time she'd been 'furloughed,' but she was pretty sure it didn't involve Google Classroom. Carla's toilette had been a little more complicated.

After the most perfunctory of showers - she was more of an evening bath girl herself - (not that she could even remember having had one of those recently) she had studied her dressing room with a mixture of nostalgia and panic. It seemed unlikely that she would be wearing any of her carefully curated spring clothes any time soon. The pastel cashmeres, soft suede Manolo flats and neat Valentino swing coats looked like costumes for a play to which she'd long ago lost the script. She rarely wore trousers anyway and the only footwear suitable for the kind of walking Seb had in mind, was a pair of old leather boots she last remembered seeing in the old house. In the end, she'd opted for jeans and a baggy Agnona sweater that she'd purchased in Capri of all places, together with the co-ordinating mink jacket.

More incredible still, was to recall that on their return to England from that trip, Seb had played polo in a charity tournament for which he'd flown over forty-eight horses from his farm in Palm Beach. *Forty-eight!* Carla shook her head. That time seemed as outlandish as the life they were living now. She'd winced at her reflection in the mirror. Her tie-dye hair was scraped back in a scruffy bun, and her face was parchment-white.

"And do you know who wrote about this place?" asked Seb as they trudged along the narrow muddy path in single file.

Carla had been outside so little recently, that she squinted in the bright sunlight, weaving her way, shielding her eyes. She was shocked at the change from the early days of lockdown when the place had been deserted. From what she could see now, the countryside was heaving with people desperate to exercise. In the distance, St. Catherine's Hill was crawling with ramblers. Every few minutes, they were forced to step back onto the bank (full of nettles) to allow people to pass - women joggers (the majority), cyclists (pests), and older couples who reacted as though she had the plague.

"Jane Austen?" said Alfie. They had just passed the house on College Street in which she had died.

"Good guess," said Seb. "But no. Carla?"

Carla shrugged. The path had widened, once they'd gone through a final turn-style, onto an even muddier field. Her supposedly waterproof boots squelched as they waded through sodden grass. On their right, the ancient building of the Hospital of St. Cross (Almhouse for Noble Poverty) was mellow grey stone against a cerulean blue sky. An avenue of poplars lay straight ahead of them.

"It was Keats," said Seb after a while with a *'ah ha! I've told you something you didn't know!'* look. "He wrote *Ode to Autumn* inspired by his daily walks here and around Winchester. Amazing to think that we're doing the same some two-hundred years later. He also told a friend that the air is worth 'sixpence here.'"

"Or one's life," muttered Carla thinking of the panting, sweating joggers happily shedding respiratory droplets willy nilly. When she felt safe and far enough away from them, she inhaled deeply, feeling brighter with every lungful. Even Alfie, for all his initial apathy, had picked up a stone and was skimming it along the water. Some ramblers wore masks, others turned their backs sullenly, if they came too near. Only the dogs seemed blissfully oblivious (if a trifle exhausted by so many walks) of all the frenzy around them. It was spring in all its glory. There was a delicious scent of wisteria and above them, a Chantilly fan of greenery protected them from the hot sun. Carla turned towards it - a veritable *gira sol* - the Spanish for sunflower popping into her head. *'Gira'*- to turn, *'sol'*- sun. Nothing at that moment mattered quite so much as the rays on her face, the gradual thawing of her heart.

"Come on!" urged Seb. "We've a while to go."

"Where to?" said Alfie, not unhappily.

They turned down the paved road that led to the farm. With that part of the M3 extension finally completed, the through road had been blocked off. Instead of carrying along the footpath up to St. Catherine's Hill, Seb turned right.

"You'll see," he said. "It's a surprise."

"OK," said Carla. "Lead on, we'll follow, won't we Alfie?"

After a short distance, a path edged with bulrushes, wound its way under the motorway towards the river. Soon after, amidst a meadow of wild flowers: poppies, daisies and hemlock, they came across a dozen dozing cattle. They could also see the spire of the village church in the distance, and as they approached Compton Lock, there was a rush of water. Carla shook her head.

"I'm embarrassed to say that I never realized you could walk along the river to Twyford."

"That's what happens when you don't walk anywhere," said Seb, placidly.

She stopped. "It's beautiful." And it was, in a quiet, undemanding kind of way. The gentle breeze rustled the branches of the tallest trees and the shallow stream was so clear that she could count the pebbles on the river bed. She hunkered down, trailing her fingers in the water. She jolted back as a fish leapt up, shimmering in a ray of light.

"Trout?" she suggested not having a clue.

"Perch."

"Ah."

"Come on," said Seb taking Alfie by the hand. "We're not

there yet."

Alfie pulled away his hand. "Can I have your phone?" he asked.

"Nope," said Seb. "No phones today, big guy. We're going to walk and look around us and observe."

Seb might as well have told him he was about to sit a four-hour maths exam.

"Didn't bring mine either," said Carla as he looked at her pleadingly. She emptied her pockets. "See?"

"But it's boring," said Alfie tears pricking his eyes.

Seb contemplated his son with amusement. "It's not boring! I'll tell you about *boring*! When I was a kid growing up in Zim -"

"Yeah, yeah," said Alfie. "On that farm where your Dad grew coffee, somewhere near the Mozambique border."

"Yes," said Seb, pleased. "That's the one. We did have coffee but not much else. No TV, no video games, no phones, or computers, no-"

"I know," said Alfie, "but I'm a kid growing up *now*. It's different."

"Ah, but it's good for you. And patience, dear boy. I've found something that you'll enjoy. I promise."

Carla smiled encouragingly. Alfie kicked a stone. Ducks and one dirty swan played a kind of animal tag before disappearing under the weir.

"But I need to chat with my friends," persisted Alfie. "And I *do* that playing games."

"Nice try," said Seb holding a wooden gate open with his jacket sleeve so as not to make direct contact with its surface. "Your friends can wait."

They crossed a large open field, then another hugging the village green before arriving at the Assumption Churchyard with its Commonwealth graves.

"If you go on just a bit further you'll see a wide bridge," said Seb to Alfie but heading in the opposite direction. "It's more of a pontoon. You can't miss it. Go with Mummy. I won't be long."

"But where are *you* going?" said Carla suddenly roused from her stupor. It was a long time since she'd had to mind Alfie by herself.

"You'll see," said Seb jauntily. "Won't be long. Go on! Just a bit further. You'll see what I mean. "

"I don't understand," grumbled Carla. "You've dragged us here, and now you're buggering off!"

Seb turned back. He brushed her cheekbone with his thumb.

"Not buggering off," he replied softly, kissing her lightly on the lips. Her own were pressed closed. "Trust me."

10

"Trust me," Seb had said, when she'd finally got into bed that night at the Belmond Sanctuary and was sobbing her heart out, her world in disarray. It seemed that her world was often in disarray, untidy and unpredictable. He had tried to hold her. It was hard to imagine a time when to be held was heaven - to have hours, days ahead together, would have been a dream come true - not just a snatched afternoon in between dropping off one child and collecting another from school or rushing to catch a train back to Winchester from London's Waterloo. When lust had dominated their relationship through quarrels, differences, even her divorce. When she could have walked out on her family for love of him. But that was before. Now, her body was rigid with resentment, anger at both him and at herself for having relented, for having been so foolish, for not having respected herself more, for not having paced herself then, for not having waited. After all, had he wanted her enough, he too would have, should have, waited. And now, here she was waiting for a dawn that was a long time coming. Within moments, Seb was asleep, snoring with his mouth open, breathing warm air onto her face. She lay awake in the dark, making not so much a fearless inventory of herself, as a list of grievances, and with every marker, her disenchantment grew.

As soon as her phone registered 5 a.m., she rose swiftly, going back into the bathroom (it felt as though she'd spent most of the night there) and dressed with more care than usual. She opted for ivory slacks and a silk Gucci top, her uniform Tods and the cashmere poncho she'd purchased in San Pedro de Atacama the autumn before and went downstairs. Breakfast was set up in a small pretty room at the back of the hotel, an altogether softer and quieter place than the cafeteria with all its hard chrome surfaces. Large windows opened onto the lush jungle area beneath Machu Pichu - slow rising mists lifting at last to bathe palm fronds in yellow light. Pictures for the hotel's brochure ought to have been taken from this angle ...

But try as she might, Carla couldn't stem the tears streaming down her face. She'd been strong enough when she stood in the bathroom, fortified by the glaring expression on the face staring back at her. But downstairs, with the serene Peruvian eyes sliding away from hers in embarrassment, she wished she could put her head down on the table and sob her heart out. At her elbow, a silent shadow poured her tea, placed fruit in front of her, shook out her napkin before laying it gently on her lap, sympathy oozing from her every gesture. Carla sipped her hot drink, salt tears mingling with the odd tea leaf. Her stomach churned. She couldn't eat a thing. Pan pipes played the ubiquitous South American music, aggravating her headache with every beat. Everything seemed surreal. *'What a difference a day made'* - crooned a Latina - *'twenty-four little hours brought the sun and the flowers where there used to be rain.'* The accent alone would have made the song completely hilarious had Carla been feeling remotely playful. She listened to the words again. In her case, it was the complete reverse.

She must have stayed at breakfast a long time - other guests came and went all (unlike Carla) in various combinations of jungle attire. Some met guides paid to accompany them on the long trek up to the Sun Gate, some, having come to the end of their stay, waited to catch the bus down to Aguascalientes. And then, just as she was finally ready to leave, she spotted Seb. Which wasn't difficult. He was the only man wearing a hat indoors. Carla tried to make herself invisible, shrinking low in her chair. But he'd seen her and was exuberant rushing towards her. Everything about him was fresh. He was fresh from a good night's sleep, fresh in beautifully laundered clothes, fresh from a shave with expensive foam, fresh in an outlook that remained unchecked.

"Great news!" he announced grandly to the entire room.

Carla shrank even further.

Seb slid into the chair opposite her, removing his Akubra and placing it on the empty chair beside them. "Oh, darling," he said. "I can stay now!"

"Of course, I wanted to kill him," she'd told her girlfriends afterwards, making light of the whole affair, somehow making their entire glamorous, amazing trip acceptable to her friends because it was now tarnished and less than perfect. "Well, I got some of the money back, but it was a bit of an expensive hiccup." In fact, lovely BA had re-reimbursed her flights within hours, but she was not so lucky with the bastard taxi. It turned out that she'd booked through some call centre in Hong Kong, and they'd flatly refused to issue a refund. As had the hotel in Cusco. It could have been worse. Carla had exaggerated parts in the retelling, but not much. What she'd not said, was how gorgeous it had all been once they'd forgotten about the drama at Machu Pichu.

The train had been every bit as wonderful as she'd hoped it would be, with its Andean décor: vicuna throws, crisp linen and delicious meals. In the evenings, over cocktails in the bar, Seb had played the piano. Seb was an accomplished pianist and could also play anything by ear. He'd once hoped to make a career in music before his parents nipped that dream in the bud by sending him to the Jesuits in Harare. The other guests had all been lovely, *interesting* people and friends by the time they'd chugged through canyons and gorges. At last, they'd reached Lake Titicaca - the highest navigable lake in the world. Small motorboats ferried the guests to Uros one of sixty 'floating islands.' The Uru people had built theirs entirely from layers of *'totora'* or thick reed. Measuring half the size of a football field, the islands could be moved in deep water or to other parts of the lake if the necessary. As the boat sped on to other islets, Carla looked back trying to frame the image in her mind: the golden thatch of tiny huts and the rainbow colours of the women's skirts, casting a shimmering reflection on the water.

In Puno, armed guards had appeared suddenly out of the shadows, dissolving just as quickly before the train set off once again, for the Sumbay Caves. Eight-thousand-year old chalk drawings could be seen in the very depths of the grotto, still clean and clear on the grey pumice. The next morning, they'd climbed to see the sunrise, Belmond minions stoking a fire and brewing fresh coffee to accompany cinnamon rolls. Their final destination of Arequipa had come all too quickly. Known as 'the white city' because of its gleaming ivory stone, it was resplendent with gracious plazas and elegant palm trees. In the end, their trip had indeed been magical. But trust? Trust was not something she would ever apply to Seb, not after what had happened. Not Aguascalientes - that was a mere blip. No, what had happened before.

*

"Now where?" asked Alfie tetchily. "*Mum!*" he bellowed when she didn't reply.

"Er ... sorry."

"You weren't listening!"

She'd been miles away. He was right. "Dad said it wasn't far."

Seb had vanished behind a row of lilac bushes but she and Alfie continued down the path which soon widened onto a low flat bridge just as Seb had said it would.

"Oh," said Carla in delight as Alfie sprang past her, throwing her an elated grin. A rope swing hung from a branch of a sprawling willow tree. The freshly mown grass beneath was speckled with dappled sunshine.

"Can I swing?" said Alfie kicking off his trainers.

"Swing or swim?" smiled Carla.

"Isn't it too cold? I thought you said you couldn't feel your fingers before."

"Was fine," she mumbled.

"Liar!" grinned Alfie launching himself onto the rope and squealing with delight as he swung far over the river. His feet barely skimmed the water's edge before he jumped onto dry land.

Carla sank onto the grass, stretching out her legs in front of her. It was utterly tranquil. Twyford was a lovely village, but the constant hum of M3 traffic and the whistle from trains made it a noisy place. Today, there were no trains or cars and the sky was pristine; not a single track marked its vast expanse of blue. It was hard to imagine hundreds of planes mothballed at airports around the world. Suddenly, the tweet of birds: robins, finches and even a buzzard as it swooped down to its prey, broke the silence. Carla too kicked off her shoes. The sun was making her drowsy, and gradually she sank closer to the ground becoming more and more supine. She wiggled her toes, cleared the odd jagged twig from under her back, observed tiny ants crawl over her fingers, felt her shoulder blades open and closed her eyes. Alfie's figure became smaller and smaller as he spun away from her…

"Where's Alfie?" Seb was standing above her, his lips fleshy with anger. Unlike most people's (hers included) whose mouths became thinner, pursed even, when they were cross, Seb's became puffy. It was always a tell-tale sign.

Carla looked up dazed. Had she fallen asleep? She must have done, as she'd not heard Seb approach. But it can't have been for long, surely? Seb had dropped a bag of groceries: a bottle of rosé, strawberries and a baguette, by her feet.

"Oh, how lovely!" she said. "Are we having a picnic?"

"Never mind that," said Seb briskly. "Where's Alfie?"

She sat up. "I-I don't know. He was here a moment ago, swinging…" Carla jumped up suddenly fully alert, fully aware of what she was saying, of where they were, of the river, gentle enough but gathering momentum as it swirled past. It no longer appeared benignly pleasant but menacing and unknown.

"But he won't have gone far. He wouldn't. He's a strong swimmer," she said panic gripping her.

"He'll have to be," said Seb grimly. "Let's just hope he hasn't fallen in."

"B-but it's so calm here," she stammered. "*Was* ... calm. Not deep and-"

"There are sluices every few yards at this bend," said Seb orienting her shoulders. "Take a look around you. There!" He turned her jerkily, as though she were an unwieldy mannequin. "And there." Now that he pointed them out, there were large signs, warning of death by drowning, that she'd not noticed earlier.

"He'd have cried out. I'd have heard him. I know I would."

Seb spun around, kicking the shopping.

"Would you? Really? You're so wrapped up in yourself, I'm surprised you hear anything!"

Carla's hand went to her throat. "That's not true," she whispered while her entrails turned in on themselves, her heart thumping painfully. "I -I."

Seb was shaking with anger.

"You - you what? *What* have you been doing exactly? I mean apart from sleeping and putting our son's life in danger!" He was shouting now, shaking with anger. "A quarter of a million people have volunteered to help support those around them but you sure as hell aren't one of them! I repeat. What the hell *do* you do?"

Carla cast her mind back, struggling to think of one distinguishing feature to separate the weekdays from the weekends but drew a blank. The past few weeks were a blur, a haze of sleepless, sweat-soaked nights followed by endless, listless days.

"I - I've been taking care of the family," she said feebly.

"We both know that's not true." His arms gestured wide. "Clearly!"

He pulled out his phone. "We're wasting precious time! Start looking while I phone the police."

Carla hesitated, instinctively reaching for her own phone before remembering she'd left it at home.

"Go!" he barked. "Now!"

Carla shot over the bridge to the other side of the bank, calling her son's name. *Please God!* she prayed. *Please, God.* Carla had been brought up a Catholic, and the far-reaching finger of guilt was never far away although it was a long time since she'd heard mass, a long time since she'd believed, full stop. But now she started a mantra, a prayer repeated again and again as though repetition were enough for it to answered. And then she started bargaining - listing all that she would do if He spared - if he *found* Alfie. She'd begin by with the practical things like washing her hair. She'd reply to all the messages that were clogging her answering service, starting with those from her aged mother. She'd volunteer to help out. Seb was right on that score.

Surely, there was *something* she could do to help out locally. She'd be nice, she'd be kind. She'd - oh, God, what a tawdry mess she was - *always* blaming Seb for *that*. Yet here she was, no better than him at all and putting their son's life in danger into the bargain. And all caused by her laziness, lack of attention and straightforward neglect. On the other hand, of course, it *was* Seb's fault - all of it. If it weren't for what had happened, she'd be a different person, more together, on top of things. *Blame it all you like on him, kid! But this one's on you,* said a little voice of conscience. This is *your* bad - she hated the expression, but it was true. *My bad - no one else's. Besides, you went ahead and got married. You had a choice. You made a commitment, and you stayed.*

Carla ran on, brambles shredding her shins, roses tearing at her hair and cheeks. Blinded by tears, she continued down the towpath calling for Alfie. There wasn't another soul about: no one walking a dog, not a single murmur from the cottages that backed onto the river, not even the odd dead mole to disrupt the picture-perfect country scene. Or complete it. Eventually, when she could go no further, Carla stopped. Hands-on knees, she bent double to catch her breath. *I'll do anything God,* she vowed. *Anything at all. I'll give up ...* She did a quick stock-take. OK. Yes. Big gulp. Deep breath. *Clothes ... I'll give up clothes.*

And with that promise, the spinning stopped, the panic subsided. She caught sight of her reflection in the river as she straightened. She looked half-demented with her wild hair and scratched face. Anyone would think she'd been attacked. She wished she had been. She'd have gladly swapped places, assuming the evil that might have befallen Alfie. Alfie. His name caught in her throat. She'd shouted so much her voice was hoarse. She was a lousy mother. What was she thinking, allowing her baby to go about half-dressed, unwashed, unsupervised with no regard to his mental health or well-being?

And *how* had she fallen asleep? She hadn't even been drinking - not that that would have been an excuse, but it would have been something. She was just so tired the whole time. She slept so badly that she wandered half dead through the days, with no release from the build-up of pressure in her head. What was the matter with her? Why couldn't she pull herself together? Seb had. He seemed to be coping pretty well, actually. But then he hadn't the *before* to contend with. His older brother called him every day. He was still adored. But then Dom didn't *know*. Carla resented that. She resented Seb's intact relationships despite what he'd done, while hers with those she cared about most, were in tatters. And only because she had chosen to stay silent, chosen to forgive. That was the crux. She had chosen to forgive but she was paying the price. And the price was guilt. Physically she was there, but not mentally. She wasn't engaged. She'd not put it behind her at all. And because of her weakness, God was punishing her by taking Alfie.

Another sob caught in her throat. She stumbled, fell headlong into a cowpat. Her nostrils filled with mud and earwigs and the fluffy, seed head of a dandelion. *Taraxacum* - large genus of flowering plants - she said it aloud, spontaneously. How extraordinary that the name should come to her after all these years. But then translation for pharmaceutical companies had once been her bread and butter. When she was young and hopeful and together. For the very short time that she'd been any of those things. For a moment, she lay prone. *Oh, Alfie*, she prayed. *Be sensible! Be safe until we find you!* She pulled herself to her feet, wiping her face with the edge of her sleeve. She called his name a final time and then retraced her steps. Violet irises and pond sedge brushed against her shoulder - a mallard, bottom-up, half-hidden amongst its reeds. She quickened her pace, to a slow jog. It took her just a few minutes to find her way back to the flat bridge. And then through a tangle of marsh marigolds, she heard the voices.

11

Carla couldn't help thinking that momentous moments were defined by the before and after, that wrinkle in time, that nanosecond that could never later be retrieved from a shield of memory perforated with holes. Some heralded joy, others tragedy. She remembered being in labour with Alfie, grunting alone, unaided, as she walked the corridors hearing the cries of new-borns in other rooms and wishing herself on the other side of that pain frontier. She told herself that if she could only ride with it, she would come through, that her will was all that mattered. There would, and could only be, one outcome. But now? As she ran towards the future, as she stepped over the pebbled path swatting away a large red damselfly, she knew there were two possible outcomes. One was too hideous to contemplate, the other a minor crease, a kink. But she did not have a moment *into* the future - across a new and terrible threshold. She did not have the luxury of being at the end of her life, or of hindsight, to comfort her. She had the now. Time was an illusion, a deception. And so, she stopped running altogether, to slow the inevitable, to give God or serendipity, time to cast in her favour. To show her clemency. To spare her.

And as she caught her breath, took deep shuddering gulps of air - air that in happier times she might have noted for its water-mint scent - the past rushed towards her, in a series of stark, vivid stills. There were choices along the way; there had always been those, but there was also timing and fate. Crucially, there was the fact that Angus had chosen not to return to the UK from abroad for the christening of a good friend's child but that Seb had. Most important of all, and the point from which there would be no return, was the simple question Seb had asked her and to which she had given an even simpler answer.

*

The weather that week was cold and stormy, but if the weather was inclement in England, it was all the more so in Siberia - Ykaterinburg to be exact. Angus, pulled out of recent retirement, had been asked to head up a new branch of his consultancy firm and had already been living there for a year. Carla was astounded when he'd told her that he (followed by a muttered 'they') would be moving to Russia. "But I thought you were looking for part-time work in *Salisbury*!" she'd faltered the morning after one of his benders when he'd finally woken up and come down to breakfast. "Oh, Carla, Carla," he'd said pityingly, annunciating the words very slowly as though she were not only deaf but stupid too. "How to explain? Let's see, what analogy? OK. Say, I was a *pilot* and not just *any* pilot but a *Concorde* pilot. A *Concorde* pilot simply doesn't fly *737s*..."

But Carla didn't see, or rather she did, all too clearly. Angus had muttered something along those lines when he'd stumbled into the kitchen of their Wiltshire home in the early hours of the morning. She was often awake then - not that Angus ever noticed. It was the only time after the twins had gone to bed, when she could read uninterrupted. At first, she'd been alarmed by the taxi's headlights bobbing up and down the tree-lined drive. Angus often stayed away, rarely affording her the courtesy of letting her know his plans. Besides, he was always so drunk when he got home that she preferred it when he did.

Now, she hurried to unbolt the front door and turn on the hall light before scampering back to her book. She hoped Angus would go straight up to bed. But he didn't, nor was he alone when he staggered into the kitchen. She wasn't sure who was more astonished, herself or the stunned taxi driver who followed him in. "I didn't think it was this far," said the poor man pitifully, virtually expiring over the AGA, adding, "he said I could have some coffee." Angus responded to this with an affronted air, as though he'd never seen the man before in his life. His eyes swirled, closing and reopening so slowly that Carla thought he'd actually fallen asleep in between blinks. But he came to, throwing back his head with a snort and then, as though remembering himself and who he was, becoming magnanimous in the wake of such an absurd request. "Coffee?" he'd said his voice faltering. He waved vaguely in the air as if conjuring up any number of minions, then seemingly genuinely perplexed when they didn't materialize. When his gaze fell on Carla, he seemed even more mystified. "Oh, it's you ..." he said at last, triumphant at having recognised her. The bewildered taxi driver looked from one face to the other for clarification.

"It's absolutely fine," said Carla to the driver, ignoring Angus. "Of course, you can have some coffee."

"Yes, yes," agreed Angus wearily as though she'd relieved him of some onerous burden. He held on to the dresser, and for a terrible moment, Carla thought he might actually keel over, taking the crockery with him. He made a final backwards lurch before grasping a corner edge steadying himself. Coffee cups, display plates and the large teapot with a lid in the shape of a crab apple, all rattled precariously.

Carla closed her eyes, but when she opened them again, miraculously nothing had broken, and Angus was removing his tie by yanking it halfway around his neck. It was nothing to what she was tempted to do to him. "Russia," was all he said. "We're moving to Russia."

Carla had taken a moment to process his words. Angus had an uncanny ability to talk sense even at his most drunk. Later, when they'd tried mediation, she had seen him crawl into a building, holding onto the walls for support (much as he was doing now) but come the meeting, he would snap to it demonstrating those sharp, incisive negotiating skills for which he was famous. Even consumed by drink, the enormity of his intellect was impressive. In 'vino veritas' and all that. But he was neither articulate nor erudite now. Nor listening. In fact, he seemed to have forgotten where he was entirely. With a pained expression, he looked around him, registering unfamiliar surroundings. Concentrating intently, he'd propelled his heavy body forward, hanging on to the door frame with both hands, pausing to look over his shoulder before exiting not followed by a bear but a glare - hers. He'd left her with the surreal feeling that he'd been an unhappy figment of her imagination. Had it not been for the very real presence of a stranger in her kitchen at 3 a.m., she might have believed that she'd imagined the whole exchange.

"So, where did you find him?" said Carla putting on the kettle to make the man strong black coffee and pushing the biscuit tin towards him. She couldn't bring herself to refer to Angus as 'her husband.' She was ashamed of him and hated his arrogance, the fact that his name, the way he spoke, his altogether patrician manner somehow let him off - allowed him to get away with (increasing) erratic behaviour. The infuriating thing was that it did. Most of the time. Angus clearly had his demons, but for men like him, his privileged background had undoubtedly smoothed his way.

"Don't tell me you've driven from Winchester?" She pursed her lips when the driver didn't answer. *Okaaay...* she thought. The Waterloo train was direct, sometimes there were changes, but Angus usually left his car at the station and drove the forty-five minutes home. They lived equidistant between Southampton and Salisbury, but he preferred the drive East. If he'd been drinking, he left the car overnight at the station and got a taxi home. It meant that Carla had to drive him into town in the morning. "Not Southampton? Don't tell me he fell asleep on the train? It happens," she chattered on reaching for her pretty Dorset Pottery mugs and motioning for the man to sit down. He looked exhausted.
"Actually, Southampton is quite a regular event. He's ended up in Brighton before. Once he went all the way to Manchester - didn't even notice! Mad, isn't it?" Her forced laugh was high-pitched verging on the hysterical. God, she was so tired of it all.

The driver stared at her as though 'mad' was the least of it.

"Winchester!" The man took two biscuits, cramming them both into his mouth. "If only! Nah, Missus," he scoffed. "Picked up the guvnor in the King's Road and himself owes me £350 for the fare."

And so, it was that Russian weather, not drink, was what had prevented Angus from travelling back the night she met Seb. Carla wasn't surprised. When she'd first googled the website for Ykaterinburg, it had made her giggle. Written without prepositions, it suggested that the visitor to the region would drop down dead with cold on first stepping foot on the tarmac. Nor was she sorry that he couldn't make it home.

When she'd recovered from the shock and then the realisation that Angus wasn't actually asking her and the twins to go with him to Russia, she'd adapted very quickly to living alone. She had felt liberated; no more to dealings with drunken apparitions (and disappearances), no more drunken rages, no more being woken up at odd hours or not being able to go to sleep in the first place because she was too upset to settle, no more asking him to collect the children only to discover hours later they were still waiting for him, no more Christmas Eves coming back from mass to find that he'd opened all their presents, no more watching him try to carve the turkey with a spoon.

Instead, she had enrolled Tom in weekly boarding and herself with a translation agency. Oh, the joy of having work to do - proper work, work that gave her pleasure! For the first time in years, she felt calm. She'd attended a few Al-Anon meetings - the support group for the spouses and families of alcoholics - but at the time her inner rage had found no outlet. It was no wonder that those do-gooders could sit quietly holding hands, nodding sagely at the newcomer's face of woe - *their* alcoholic was in recovery, striving to get better! What did you do when your spouse/partner refused to acknowledge they even had a problem? Wouldn't talk about anything at all and never about anything as pedestrian as 'feelings'? So, she'd given up on her oh-so-serene sponsor and buried herself in work. She'd found all the serenity and peace of mind she could possibly have dreamed of by being removed physically from Angus. Having him live in a completely different country suited her perfectly. Him too, she suspected. Even so, it was a kind of fate that determined Angus stay there now - a kind of fate that decreed she accept the invitation to be godmother to a friend's new-born daughter. And another fate entirely that decided Seb should be the baby's godfather.

They'd met over the font. That's what Seb liked to say, and she did too at the beginning. Except that it wasn't completely accurate. They'd actually first 'met' a few days after Natasha was born. Angus had been on another bender - the longest to date. Carla hadn't seen him at all since he'd agreed to collect Tom from school - only he'd never turned up. It wasn't the first time that sort of thing had happened, but it was the first time that Carla had involved the police. They'd come to the house, stayed with her, looked around his bedroom, put out calls and then come back to her with the update that they'd traced his car. To a Premier Inn in Plymouth. She couldn't praise the police enough. They were exemplary - considerate and tactful. Yet 'thank you' seemed somehow wrong in the face of such news. And there was the open question of what Angus had been doing in Plymouth, in a Premier Inn, away from home. But by that point, Carla no longer cared. Wasn't even curious. Shaken, indeed, from a night spent prowling the house, alternating between making the police and herself cups of tea, but no longer gutted, no longer brittle with hurt and so much worse, no longer hopeful that things might get better. Natasha, the mother of a friend of Sophie's, had given birth that morning to a little girl called Xenia. Carla and Natasha had also become good friends. Natasha was already home and wanted to see her.

Carla hadn't hesitated. She'd rushed to the nearest florist, popped into a children's boutique she knew of in Stockbridge and sped to Northington Park. She'd raced past The Grange and down the bumpy unmarked track that led to Natasha's gingerbread cottage. Already she felt miles away from Angus, even the twins.

"Christ!" said Natasha when Carla appeared at the bedroom

door. "You look like you've had the baby, not me!"

"Thanks," said Carla, but it was true. She caught sight of herself in the dressing table mirror. She was as white as Natasha's sheet, with black shadows under her eyes.

On the other hand, Natasha lounging on her pretty bed was the very picture of health - glowing skin and hair, shining eyes.

"Xenia?" riposted Carla when Natasha told her the baby's name. "To match Xavier?"

Natasha made a face. "A bit twee. But you know how we like our Russian names."

"Yes, funny that," said Carla deadpan, sinking onto the end of the bed as Natasha unveiled her new-born infant.

"Oh, she's beautiful!" exclaimed Carla. And she was. Even at less than a day old, Xenia was an elegant baby, fine-featured and delicate. Carla's heart flipped.

"You can hold her," said Natasha reading her thoughts.

Carla scooped up the feather-light little bundle feeling her pulsating neck against hers, the little twists as the baby stretched, moving towards the light, her slow rhythmic breathing. Carla wanted to hold her forever.

"I'd forgotten what it's like, to have a new baby," said Carla a crack in her voice. "So precious. Such a responsibility but there's nothing more important."

And that's when Natasha had asked Carla to be Xenia's godmother.

"If I'm not much mistaken," she added, looking out of the

window. "Talk about timing! That's the godfather arriving now."

"Oh?" Carla hadn't even looked up, her face lightly pressed against Xenia's, mindful of the baby's soft skull but drinking in her lovely, clean, talc baby smell - soothed by it, made hopeful.

"Yeah," said Natasha going all London cool on her. "He's Xav's best friend. He's called Sebastian Cave. A Rhodesian - sorry *Zimbabwean* but he's been living in America. He was at university with Xav. He was a Rhodes scholar, and yes, that pun did the rounds. I *think* he may have dated Pam but never quite sure."

Natasha mentioned her older sister. It had ended amicably, but Natasha warned her to be wary of Seb's charm. He went out with *everyone*. He was insatiable - a total playboy. *Thanks again*, thought Carla - *first I'm married and second even were I free - I'm not 'everyone.'* Natasha's voice faded to a steady monotone. Carla hardly heard, focusing all her attention on the baby: her little wrinkled wrists, uncannily long nails, and bow legs, bunched up against a nappy that seemed far too large for her tiny frame. She heard random words: 'polo, private plane, doesn't have to work, plays the piano, several girlfriends - one a household name surely, you've heard of?' And the current favourite, apparently a six-foot tall Azeri.

"Where *is* that?"

"Azerbaijan." Natasha was pleased Carla didn't know.

"Sounds like something out of *Gulliver's Travels*," said Carla.

"No, it doesn't!" said Natasha feigning offence. "He's super glamorous!"

"Of course, he is," said Carla quickly. "If he's going to be this princess's godfather."

But she wasn't serious, nor was she interested in knowing more. Carla only wished she could slip out of the house without having to say hello to anyone downstairs. Her spirits sank at the thought of going home, but she had stayed out long enough and took Natasha's yawn as a sign that it was time for her to go. Reluctantly, she handed over the baby. As she leant over to kiss her friend goodbye, Natasha caught her hand.

"Things will work out," she said. "You know you can always talk to Mummy." She meant her own.

Carla froze. "I'm fine," she said stiffly. "Just fine." She never talked about her personal life, never unburdened herself to anyone, not even Natasha although her friend had occasionally witnessed drunken scenes and had been sympathetic. Her own father was an alcoholic and Natasha had once told her that her mother had temporarily left him - hence the suggestion that she might be someone Carla could confide in. But if this was an invitation to swop drink related stories, Natasha was disappointed. Carla had learned her lesson.

She'd let slip once, something about Angus's drinking to a new friend only to have that friend cut her the next day. The friend had said it was nothing personal, but she didn't 'know people' with complicated family lives and wanted to keep it that way. Stung to the quick, Carla had recoiled burrowing back into herself never to divulge anything again. She didn't point out that to her mind, a friendship worked both ways, that she'd spent hours and hours listening to this same friend bemoan her childless state. But she let it go. *'The people that matter won't mind, the people that mind don't matter.'* Or as her mother had advised, quoting Confucius or some such, *'Laugh and the world laughs with you, cry, and you cry alone.'* But when Carla had finally left Angus, she was surprised to learn that most of her friends knew about his drinking anyway.

Carla closed the door softly behind her, overcome by an overwhelming brooding sensation - her whole being yearned for another baby. She'd never felt such an impulse before, not even with the twins. She paused for a moment on the landing before slowly descending the stairs. Portraits from a grander home lined the walls: peripatetic collections from another age. Elsewhere, black and white school photographs of Xavier's father and then Xavier himself at the same age, were crammed on the top of bookshelves and occasional tables. Dusty team pictures chronicled sporting prowess: cricket, football and rugby. As the boy grew, his hobbies extended to the country pursuits of the landed gentleman: shooting, fishing and hunting. The women were not ignored. Silver framed, velvet-backed photographs abounded of elegant women in neat, figure-hugging habits riding side-saddle. These beautiful creatures completed their own social circuits at Ascot and Henley. They could be seen sprawling on the grass dressed in glorious rainbow-coloured silks at Glyndebourne, parading in fantastic costumes at masquerade balls or wrapped in lustrous furs at winter parties.

Later, when social distancing became the norm, Carla and Natasha would marvel that such gatherings had ever been possible. Now, peering closely, it would seem that a photograph couldn't be framed unless it included a backdrop of a stately home or Capability Brown designed garden, or failing either of those, a small plane. Carla had forgotten that Xavier's father used to fly the family everywhere in a pretty little Cessna until the morning he crashed it on his way to

Biarritz. Thankfully, he'd been alone. Natasha had once hinted there was more to the story. There'd been gossip about a mistress. More recent photographs showcased Natasha's children - the girls, when they were younger wore Liberty print smock dresses, the only boy was in rompers. Order and assurance emanated from every photograph. This was a family acutely aware of its provenance - confident of where it was heading. The latest baby, Xenia, was one more addition in this long line of continuity. There was something in this family's fecundity that made Carla's own feel weedy and impoverished. It only made her yearning all the more acute.

If the upper floors were shrine-like in honouring the past, the ground floor catapulted the family into the present. At first glance, the corridor with its tasteful, calming fusion of white and grey textiles was unremarkable. It was only up-close that the wallpaper revealed itself to be of cavorting monkeys. The family sitting room didn't disappoint either. The theme there was zebras, while gold elephants graced the walls of the drawing room. Carla went into the kitchen, opening the door to a cacophony of sound and colour. Norah Jones's inconsequential crooning was drowned by the din of pots and pans and general chatter. Xavier seemed oblivious to his children baking around him. Standing at the island, he deftly moved his PC out of the line of fire when sticky cake mixture splashed his way. From time to time, he blew his fringe out of his eyes or wiped his glasses clean.

The Austrian au pair with her doughy plump folds and blonde ringlets and wearing her own version of a dirndl, folded clothes in neat, colour-coded piles. Carla smiled inwardly. Natasha always seemed to find the caricature of a nationality personified in her help. This one really was a veritable Apfelstrudel. Her only son, Sasha, stood by the Aga dismantling his bicycle, a half-eaten bacon sandwich on the griddle beside him. No one looked up as Carla entered, and she might have managed to slip away unnoticed. No one that is, except for the man lolling in a chair in the corner. As aware of the din, as the others around him were oblivious, dressed in white jeans, boots and a polo shirt, was Seb.

Carla was rumbled, as she tried to tiptoe past. Xavier greeted her in his usual vague manner, but the children squealed with delight at the arrival of a newcomer who wasn't going to ignore them completely. Proudly, they showed her one of the cakes they'd made earlier which was cooling on the counter. The co-godparent Seb appraised her legs as he would a pony's. His own were stretched out in front of him as though he were sunning himself in a deck chair - one arm languidly skimming the floor. Suddenly, some unknown urge prompted him to jump up. "Off!" he announced. "We're off to play polo!" She'd never have guessed. Xavier was evidently going with him for the word 'polo' seemed to produce a Pavlovian response. He snapped shut his Mac and grabbed his keys from the bucket of spares on the far side of the island.

Carla marvelled he was able to find anything in amidst the general paraphernalia of cookbooks, vanilla pods, baking tins, Lego, A-level Geography, candles, Tesco Strawberry Laces and a small statue of a Terracotta Warrior. Almost out the door, Seb hesitated. "So, you could come," he threw over his shoulder as casually as he had knotted the cashmere sweater around his neck and pointing at Carla, just in case the au pair or any of the children misinterpreted the invitation. Carla felt herself flush. Pointing at her? *Seriously?* There was no, "Would you like to? Can I introduce myself?" or even "And you must be?" Carla was a bit fed up with being considered as an accessory, an appendage, a nonentity. "So," she'd mimicked him. "No, thanks,". His eyebrows shot up in surprise. Polo players were accustomed to women falling in a swoon at the sight of white jeans, never mind being actually spoken to! But she wasn't most women, and she didn't like horses or the 'sport of kings.' What an arrogant pair! She thought as Xavier and Seb vanished up the drive in his Porsche, gravel and dust splaying in all directions. No wonder they were such good friends.

12

Carla ran on, only stopping for breath when she'd reached the grassy knoll where she'd fallen asleep earlier, and Alfie had been playing. She bent down, hands on knees and then straightened slowly. The voices seemed to have dissipated in the quiet air, and there was no one about. Without her phone, she had no option but to retrace her steps and return home across the fields. Once she'd gathered her strength, she started running again as fast as she could towards Compton Lock, half expecting to see police fishing out the body of her son. But there was no one there either, and it wasn't until she was on the home stretch, racing past the Mill that she saw a person - an old lady hunched over on a park bench.

"Are you all right?" she asked breathlessly. She glanced at the woman, grey hair in two thick plaits, flower-patterned skirt, tank top and stout walking boots. The hands clutched in her lap were dirty, the nails caked with soil. Maybe she'd been gardening. A second glance confirmed that she wasn't nearly as old as Carla had initially thought - this side of sixty rather than a decade older. But she looked at Carla wide-eyed, recoiling from her in genuine fear, shrinking even further when Carla instinctively took a step towards her. "You haven't seen a small boy, have you? Or a tall man with dark hair - a bit …" She did her best to avoid staring at the ring through the woman's eyebrow. "A bit hippyish?"

The lady stared at her stonily. She was probably just lonely, thought Carla. She looked lonely. Or maybe she was deaf.

Carla shrugged, tried one last time, smiling pleasantly. "It's hard though isn't? Being separated from friends and -"

The woman looked up. "My husband died a few weeks ago," she mumbled.

Carla was immediately sympathetic, and if it hadn't been for the two metre social distancing rule, would have sat down on the bench beside her.

"I'm so sorry," she said gently. "How difficult -"

"Difficult?" she spat. "What would you know?"

The woman lifted her head belligerently. She gripped the edges of her skirt, but Carla had the impression that given half a chance, she'd have liked to give Carla a good slap. "You ask if I've seen a child? A husband? *You* aren't on your own then."

"No, I'm not, but I've lost them. We became ... separated."

"Bloody careless."

Carla was stung, but the woman was right. "A bit, yes," she agreed.

The woman was taking no prisoners, and suddenly Carla felt foolish and spoiled and somehow irrelevant. The widow leaned back, digging her hands in her pocket.

"So, you've actually no idea what it's like at all, do you?"

Carla was beginning to wish that she hadn't stopped to talk. "No, you're right," she said quietly. "I don't but I-"

"But you what?" The woman's eyes were tepid, watery, expressionless. "You felt *sorry* for me? You thought you'd risk my life by spitting at me?"

"I'm not *spitting*!" said Carla incredulously. *Talk about no good turn goes unpunished!* Another one of her mother's favourite sayings. "And I definitely don't feel sorry for you." *Who would!* "Since when was talking risking any one's life?"

The woman's look was penetrating, scornful.

"'Stay home. Save Lives.' Don't you get it?"

Stay home, stay depressed! I think lady you're the living proof! But Carla didn't say any of that. Obviously.

"We don't know enough about how the virus." A hysterical giggle rose in her throat. Everything was so surreal. This conversation, that slogan, this pandemic. Even now, at this moment, she wanted to pinch herself. Had any of it really happened? Was it actually happening? Had she really lost Alfie?

"Oh, go away, you daft cow!"

Carla gripped her fists. It was Carla's turn to want to throw a punch. She turned to walk away.

"I did see a small boy," the woman cleared her throat. "And a hippy - a really old hippy mind you."

"What?" Carla swung around instantly, forgetting her irritation. "When? Are you sure? The boy too? Are you sure there was a boy?" She'd let the 'old hippy' bit go, but she needed to be clear about Alfie. "Did you *really* see a child so high?" Carla held her hand to her chest. "He was wearing…" Christ, what *was* he wearing? "A t-shirt with a picture of the Panama Canal!" She said it triumphantly, making a circular motion in front of her chest. Carla had bought both her boys the same style (different colours) on their recent trip.

"Don't know about that," said the woman withdrawing into herself again. "Don't know at all."

No, I don't suppose you do. Carla took a step towards her. The woman almost fell off the bench in panic.

"Oh, never mind," said Carla. "Stay safe."

Carla hurried on, praying that the woman was right. She continued with her silent mantra to spare Alfie and was still praying when she squeezed through the last wooden gate by Winchester College's New Hall. But the encounter with the widow had unnerved her. It had made her realise that in her need to blame Seb for the past, she'd taken a great deal for granted in the present. The widow was right to be bitter. She didn't *have* to talk to Carla. Why should she? She'd been sitting minding her own business when Carla had burst in on her. After all, the woman had lost something - *someone* precious - permanently lost them. Carla had lost hers (hopefully only temporarily) out of her own inattention, her own self-absorption. She'd been thoughtless with those around her - less careful of those she loved than the consideration she gave to her expensive clothes. She'd had happiness handed to her on a plate and not known what to do with it. There was another realisation. She couldn't carry guilt with regards to her older children with her forever. She adored them, had failed them, but it was time to move on. To 'be' as Sophie kept reminding her. What Carla had to resolve, however, was a healthier, steadier relationship with her daughter. Somehow, Carla's happiness couldn't always depend on Sophie's changeable acceptance. It was eating away at Carla, preventing her from giving her all to Alfie and yes, even to Seb.

Carla had tried to convince herself that she had drawn a line over the past, but she hadn't really. She talked in grand terms about forgiveness, but she hadn't forgiven Seb, not for a moment. How arrogant of her to even think forgiveness was hers to give! The only person she could genuinely forgive was herself. And she was a long way from doing that.

The path had become an obstacle race of raised gnarled and twisted roots. As Carla carefully picked her way through the tangled undergrowth, she made new pacts and promises. Now, she was not only praying for Alfie's safety, but promising all kinds of add-ons. She had a plan, she would change. And she would be loving to Seb, she would try and recoup some of the romance they'd once enjoyed.

Just spare me Alfie, and I will change ...

13

Carla hadn't given Seb another thought after the day she'd first seen him lolling in an armchair and this time when she entered the drawing-room, candlelight making the gold elephants virtually leap from the wallpaper, she barely noticed him at all. This time, there was no opportunity for him to loll anywhere - that was the prerogative of the dowager. Xavier and the other godparents occupied the remaining sofas and armchairs grouped around the fireplace. Natasha, in pearls and a little DVF wrap dress, was feline, her shapely dancer's leg beautifully extended. It was the leg more than the man that caught Carla's attention. She had a sixth sense where Natasha was concerned. Her interests must lie ... Carla looked again. Yes, in *his* direction. She was curious but to begin with all she could see was an outline, a large irregular shadow. He too must have arrived late because he squatted on the only available seat, a long low stool, his broad frame dwarfing the delicate furniture. Yet despite this, he seemed utterly relaxed. Carla was anything but.

At first, the twins had flatly refused to accompany her to this pre-christening supper. Natasha was a good friend but a little draconian in her views on child-rearing. Not that Carla didn't secretly agree with her on some points, but she knew that the children would be eating separately, expected to be neither seen nor heard. With Angus away, and Tom only home on weekends, Carla wanted to spend as much time with him as possible. Sophie had more than articulated her views on the matter. Carla didn't feel much like going either, so it was easy to promise an early return. They'd stay for dinner, long enough to be polite. And then just as she was hurrying the children into the car, she'd stepped back too quickly, the heel of her shoe snapping in two. Completely panicked, she'd run upstairs to change her foot-wear. She pulled off the lovely new dress that only went with the one ruined pair of shoes and began opening cupboards. *What, what, what to wear?* The pulse at her temple was throbbing, *think, think, think!* Tom sounded the horn outside, Sophie was hollering for her to hurry. They'd turned up the volume on the car radio, and the whole house seemed to be reverberating.

The car door slammed. "I'm not sitting beside him!" screamed Sophie.

Carla opened her dressing-room window, cold air rushing in. "I'm coming!" she called down, but the more she tried to hurry, the more unnerved she felt.

"Come *on!*" yelled Sophie her face turning puce. "We're already late!"

Carla rarely wore jeans, but now they seemed the simplest option. Except that without the shoes she would have worn with her dress, they were far too long. With no time to hem them, Carla took a pair of bathroom scissors and hacked off the bottom.

No, relaxed was not at all what she'd felt when she'd entered Natasha's drawing-room.

"Gin and tonic? Champagne?" said Xavier blowing the fringe from his eyes.

"Oh, here," said Natasha reluctantly when it was clear her husband was in no hurry to give their guest either. "Have a seat."

"No, don't worry," said Carla.

"Have mine," said the bulky shape but he was so hemmed in he could just about move his foot.

"She'll sit here, Seb." snapped Natasha. "What are you wearing?" she added in a stage-whisper. "I've never seen you in jeans?"

Carla tried to minimise the effect of a frayed hem by standing on one leg, flamingo-like. "Same."

But despite her bravado, Carla realised she'd got the dress code all wrong. Xavier's mother, the grand and crusty Dowager Countess of Ayling, was also wearing a dress and pearls. Still elegant at seventy-eight, she was no stranger to donning leather trousers on occasion, but celebrating the arrival of a new 'honourable' didn't merit pants of any description - definitely not denim. The other godmother - Carla acknowledged her greeting with a nod - was dressed in a demure cocktail dress - the sexiness of black lace neutralised by a white collar and cuffs. She cast an eye over Carla's wild locks with a look that implied she wasn't surprised. The other godfather was a hotelier in the Far East, French and suave and clearly gay otherwise Natasha would have been seated at *his* feet.

Uncharacteristically, Carla didn't care. She was so worn down by caring solely for the children in Angus's absence, that frizzy hair was the least of it. After the initial euphoria of his departure had worn off, Carla had soon discovered that having another adult in the house, even a drunk like Angus was better than nobody. She could seldom get the heating or hot water to work (at least not at the same time) and once she'd been scared half to death by the discovery of squirrels in the attic. She was lonely for company, someone to talk to and more importantly, someone to help comfort children who missed their father. She'd been surprised at the extent to which they did. Of course, they did. He was still their father. She was the one who nagged and scolded and had tantrums out of frustration. No one invited her out to dinner, no one invited her anywhere. Instead, she was asked to let them know when Angus was home for any length of time. As her friends' husbands repeatedly informed her, she was neither 'divorced' nor a 'widow', so how to treat her?

"No Angus?" said Xavier.

"No Angus," echoed Carla, but she suddenly felt clammy. Surely, Natasha had told Xavier that Angus was stuck in Siberia? They couldn't be expecting him? Carla would pop to the loo and try and see if there was a place set for him at the table.

"Come sit," said Seb patting the seat vacated by Natasha.

Carla hesitated. She hadn't cared for the man when she'd seen him after Xenia was born and she wasn't sure her initial opinion was going to change much now, but she sank down, clasping her knees to her chest. Eventually, Xavier handed her a glass of champagne.

She shook her head.

"Just water, thanks," she said.

Seb looked surprised. "You don't drink?"

When Angus had announced that the Concorde pilot really was off to Russia, Carla had actually burst out laughing.

"What's so funny?" he'd asked.

"You," she'd said unkindly. "Drinking as you do, you won't

last one minute in Russia."

"No?" he'd replied quietly. "We'll see."

They'd never spoken about his giving up drink as such. Over their years together, Carla had ranted and raved. She'd been particularly affronted when her doctor suggested that *she* go to Al-Anon (the cheek! *She* wasn't the one with the problem!), but none of that had done any good. If Carla so much as mentioned the word 'drink', Angus would storm out to the pub. Which was why, when the possibility of his working in Siberia became a reality she'd been stunned to learn that he'd quietly gone to see his private GP in London. She wasn't sure what the man had said or even prescribed, except that it must have been strong medication because any time so much as a drop of alcohol passed his lips, Angus was violently ill. Chocolate liqueurs were out as was cider gravy, figs in port, beef bourguignon, custards with Grand Marnier or even those delectable brownies made from prunes soaked in Armagnac. In solidarity, she'd given up too. It felt wrong to have a drink if he couldn't. But where to even begin with all of that?

"I do, I did," she corrected. "I - I sort of gave up."

Seb raised an eyebrow. He had fine, arched eyebrows she noted over deep blue eyes. The contrast with his dark hair was very sexy. But his expression when she caught him looking at her, was kind. She felt herself relax. He told her about his girlfriend - the six-foot Azeri who couldn't be there that weekend as she was seeing her children. It seemed the way these days with blended families. Children came first, he'd said. He didn't have any of his own, but he understood. And then Carla somewhat spoiled things by looking at his Prada loafers.

"Are those *wedges?*"

There was nothing more seductive Carla decided, than having a man (literally) captive at her feet, hanging on her every word. Seb was a good listener. After years of being dismissed as a complete fool by Angus, having him make strained expressions if she voiced an opinion - it was a novelty to have this stranger really listen. So that when he asked her "And you, are you happily married?" Carla hadn't hesitated.

Carla was unaware of anyone around them - not of Xavier's frosty mother not to mention Natasha's own froideur or the fact that the hyper-religious other godmother was forced to converse with the louche other godfather or that Xavier himself bored by then, had taken himself off to bed halfway through dessert. Yes, there was a spark - an electrifying, tingling, touch me spark. On the way to checking on the twins, Seb had intercepted her. Leaning against the cooker, he'd sprung up to feel the scar on her forehead - asking for an explanation. She was certain that Angus had never asked her about it - pretty certain that he'd never noticed. It had been caused by a childhood accident, but half the time Carla herself forgot about it. She found herself attracted to Seb not only physically, but because he was so easy to talk to. He had a girlfriend - the Azeri - she had Angus, there was no question of romantic involvement. Like her, Seb had grown up in another country before coming to live in the UK. At a later date, she would tease him, calling him her fellow 'Colonial'. But when she referred to some TV programme or other, to a popular drink, an antiquated turn of phrase, he knew what she was talking about. It made her feel cosy, less alone.

They talked all through drinks, dinner and coffee. Much to

the dowager's disgust, Seb had lobbed chocolates across the table aiming for her cleavage. Little chocolate stars cartwheeled through the air missing her completely. It was juvenile, but it made her laugh. And it was a long time since she had laughed.

"I hope you're better at polo!" Carla had said surprising herself at her daring.

Seb, lining up his next chocolate, had paused. "There's no fun in scoring straight away," he'd said, and she'd blushed.

At 1 a.m., her children and Natasha escorted her to the door.

"I *knew* you'd stay!" Sophie had said accusingly, climbing into the back of the car. "Why do you always have to be the last to leave?"

"I don't know," said Carla dreamily. "I rather enjoyed myself."

"Well, *we* didn't," said Sophie. Tom was non-committal. "*And* we have to come back tomorrow!"

"Wait, what?" Tom was now fully alert.

"For the actual christening, dummy."

Sophie kicked him for no good reason.

"That hurt," he said.

"Stop it," said Carla vaguely.

They whizzed through the night - a journey that on the outset had seemed tedious and lengthy, by return was quick and smooth. It was as if they were flying on winged feet. Their Queen Anne house at the end of the tree-lined drive looked particularly beautiful in the moonlight. To Carla's mind, everything that night was enhanced. The stars in a mysterious inky sky, seemed brighter than usual, tiny yet powerful pen lights accentuating the pond at the front of the house. A single deer raised a delicate hoof scraping at the ice, its breath hanging iridescent in the freezing air. Carla smiled soppily. Sophie shooting her a sideways glance wasn't taken in.

"You're weird," she said, getting out and slamming the door. Expertly, she shifted the jardinière, rooting around in the soil for the spare key.

"We'll be robbed, one day," volunteered Tom calmly.

"She knows," said Sophie. "She doesn't care."

"*She?*" said Carla unperturbed. "I do care. It's just that-"

"And we never set the alarm!"

"No, that's true."

Sophie glared. "Useless." She pushed past her mother and went into the house and straight up to bed.

Probably true too. Carla smiled. "'Nite then!" she called after her. Carla could track her daughter's route to the first floor by the number of lights switched on in her wake.

"Love you, Mum," said Tom also brushing past but pausing to lean into her. Carla hugged him.

"Love you more," she said. For a moment, she held his teenage frame. He was now as tall as she was. He'd always been such a gentle, reasonable child and ever-patient in the face of his sister's tyranny. Having said that, Carla was confident Sophie would have done anything to protect her brother if the need arose. She also knew he missed Angus desperately. She squeezed his arm. He smiled reassuringly. "It'll be OK," he said.

Carla remained outside welcoming the cold air and hoping it would cool if not her hot face, then the rush of emotions swirling through her. She was elated - on a high from having been out socially for the first time in months. For just that evening, she'd been Carla, not Angus's wife, not the twins' mother, just Carla. Most of all, it was a relief to meet someone who didn't know her story, with whom she didn't have to pretend about anything. "And you, are you happily married?" Seb had repeated the question after he'd told her about the six-foot Azeri and Carla had told Seb about Angus living in Russia. It was an obvious question, slightly contrived perhaps but not one that anyone had ever asked her before - not even her girlfriends. And when she'd answered, "No, no, I'm not," it was one of the most liberating moments of her life. She'd said it aloud, she'd admitted it to herself and to this man who knew absolutely nothing about her, that she wasn't happy.

She stretched her arms high above her head, mentally embracing the house. Feeling positive about the place wasn't always the case. There were times when she would lie awake cursing its every brick, scared rigid by the scratching sounds coming from between the walls. A few weeks before, Carla had been horrified to see mice zig-zagging across her bedroom floor. Sophie of course, because she loved all form of wildlife, had insisted Carla purchase humane traps. But because mice have an uncanny (or genius way) of finding their way back to a house, Carla had been forced to drive half a mile down the road, in her PJs (why did mice appear at night?) to release the little vermin into a neighbouring field.

Carla wasn't sure the exercise had been such a success. The very next night, she'd been woken by a mouse scampering across the room, a piece of chocolate skillfully from one of those 'nice' traps beside her bed.

But tonight, nothing mattered. As Carla followed her children into the house, she spared an affectionate thought for the sweet little mice. She didn't shudder with cold (it was only marginally warmer inside than out) as she tweaked the hall rug to cover shrinking floorboards and block the arctic blast gusting up from the cellar. She'd gone into the kitchen to boil a kettle for a hot water bottle and then taken it up to bed with her when it was ready. But she not to sleep. Curled under the duvet, her eyes felt wired open as she tried to make out familiar shapes through splinters of moonlight: a Georgian tall-boy and silk curtains billowing away from its bell-like frame, a sailing boat on the cusp of a wave in a seaside watercolour, Aubusson rugs and a window-seat in pretty gingham, had a Swedish feel. It was a beautiful, elegant room but frigid both figuratively and literally. Carla was used to being alone. Tonight, she rejoiced in her solitude and the wistful tweet of barn owls, so that she could re-live the evening over and over.

In the end, Carla must have fallen asleep only waking when it sounded as if the entire bird population had nose-dived into her window. She never minded the wood pigeons whose gentle putting she usually found soothing - this morning they seemed to be hurrying her along. She'd leapt out of bed all energy and tingling nerves and padded into her dressing room to begin the serious business of dressing.

"What are you doing?" said Sophie coming into the room moments later.

"You know that we're already late, don't you? I mean *again*?" Carla was relieved to see that unlike her, Sophie was dressed and ready, her hair swept up in a pretty updo. She looked adorable - young and fresh and appropriate in what nanny would have called her 'church' coat - a sweet little blue tweed with a velvet collar. She wore slightly clumpy heels, a feather fascinator and a fifteen-year-old cross expression.

"Where's Tom?" said Carla quickly.

"Asleep."

"My God, it's not..?" Carla grabbed Sophie's wrist, squinting to see the face on the tiny watch. "What's the time? I can't read."

"You need glasses."

"Probably. Oh, this is hopeless!" Carla stood shivering in her underwear, paralysed with indecision. This part of the house was even colder than the cellar if that were possible. All her wardrobe doors were open, drawers pulled out, the carpet strewn with garment covers from well-known fashion houses. Padded hangars conjoined in Rubik cube complexity, lay atop Balmain blazers and Gucci pinafores. The French chaise-longue was entirely covered in stiff silk faille frocks, Chanel braided jackets and gauze skirts. Fur wraps, cashmere pashminas, and geometric-patterned scarves were strewn over the carpet. For someone as obsessed with clothes as Carla was, she never had anything to wear.

Sophie stepped gingerly over the piles of clothes.

"Do you ever consider the High Street?"

"No."

Carla dragged out a brightly patterned yellow dress by *The Vampire's Wife* - it had huge sleeves, and a (very short) gathered hem. Too short. Sophie shook her head. She was right. Not only was the colour wrong, but her daughter questioned the name of the brand.

"*Are* you a *Vampire's*...?"

"Funny."

There was *Zimmerman* (too frou-frou) and *Rixo* (too much like shape-wear), a *Row* stretch scuba tube (au Jacques Cousteau), a shift by *Guerlain* (too nun-like), and a microscopic *Bottega Veneta*. That last one might have worked with an additional metre or two of material sewn along the bottom. An *Alexander McQueen* with a zillion studs looked like bondage. She picked up a leopard print *Ganni*.

"Grr!" growled Sophie. "OK, what *were* you going to wear?"

"I don't know!" wailed Carla. She had a wardrobe designed to accommodate international travel, opera and embassy parties but not country christenings.

"This is the problem when you have too much stuff." Sophie glanced disapprovingly at the discarded clothes, picking up a mohair sweater and holding it to her face. "I forgot I hate these hairy things, they always get in my eyes."

Carla took the garment out of her hands. "Mine too. Not sure why I keep it."

"You're actually turning blue!" said Sophie helpfully.

"Ah, ha!" Carla spied a *Maison Valentino* skirt poking out from under a pair of Roger Vivier flats. In red white, pink, orange and brown vertical stripes of varying dimensions, it had ever-larger circles in contrasting colours starting from the waist. Some of the strips were edged in Valentino's signature scallop finish.

Sophie's eyes widened.

"I'm thinking circus top."

"No, this is good." Carla stepped into the skirt, did up the zip and pulled on a cashmere polo.

"*He* was wearing a polo jumper," said Sophie, her tone flinty. *So, he was…* that was why probably why, subconsciously, Carla had chosen one too. She grabbed a pair of *Jimmy Choo* suede boots. "Done!"

Sophie appraised her mother tilting her head. "You look like a matryoshka doll."

Carla caught a glance of herself. "Oh, dear," she said. "I do a bit."

"You'll certainly stand out."

Goodie …

"But will this do? I kind of messed up last night."

Sophie smirked. As if implying not only on the clothes front.

"It's fine," she said. "But please tell me you're not dressing up for *him*?"

Halfway to pulling on her boots, Carla hesitated. ''I don't

know what you mean," she said primly. "I'm the godmother remember."

"Y-yes and he's the godfather." Sophie wrapped a fox stole around her shoulders. "I think I'll wear this," she said.

"Oh, darling, I was going to!"

If Carla found setting off for Natasha's the evening before stressful, it was nothing to the anxiety that consumed her as they'd approached the Park.

"You're not letting Tom bring his skateboard, are you?" Sophie had said as they screeched to a halt in front of the tiny, medieval church. *Never mind the skateboard* thought Carla, as the twins tumbled out of the car. To her dismay, Tom couldn't have looked scruffier. His hair was too long, his gaping school jacket too short. There was also something odd about it, and when Carla leaned in closer, she could see that he'd replaced missing buttons with capacitors. *On the upside* thought Carla, *at least it looks like he's been visiting the DT department.* When he bent down to adjust a bolt on the board, she also noticed he wasn't wearing any socks. Gingerly she stepped over him, standing on tippy-toe so as not to damage her skinny Choo heels. She scanned the row of parked cars - one Range Rover (the other godmother's), a Porsche (was that Seb's or the other godfather's?) and a battered Volvo (definitely Xavier's). So, one was missing unless Seb had cadged a lift, but had he even been spending the night at the Park? She couldn't remember what he'd said he was going to do.

Sophie marched on ahead, the feathers of her fascinator whipped by the wind, Tom overtaking her. "Wait, Tom!" hissed Carla, but he was already inside the vestibule, prising open the heavy oak door, his skateboard clattering on the flagstones. Partly to cover her embarrassment and partly out of habit, Carla genuflected and then with her hand halfway to crossing herself, remembered that none of that was common practice in the Church of England. Natasha, immaculate in midnight velvet Beulah, muttered her disapproval not only at their tardiness but at their theatrical entrance. Carla suppressed a giggle - there *was* something a little clown-like about them - she in her bright, dotty skirt - Tom skidding to a halt - as if they were about to perform some act. Which she supposed they were. Clearly, Natasha didn't find them quite so entertaining. Raising her eyes at the skateboard, she muttered something about 'chavyness.'

Meanwhile, nestling in her mother's arms, Xenia slept on contentedly, completely unaware of the fuss being created around her. There was a slight tug of war as Carla made a "Can I hold her?" bid but Natasha, liking the effect made by acres of antique lace cascading down the front of her velvet frock, wasn't in a hurry to relinquish her baby. The other godmother in a prim tweed coat - an adult version of Sophie's - patiently waited her turn. Using the battle for Xenia as an excuse, Carla edged her way discretely back to the vestibule. In a side pew, the twins were huddled over their phones, sharing one set of earphones. Carla motioned to her children to join Natasha's even though Sophie's black look made it very clear she'd rather eat her toenails. Carla hovered as long as she dared, but as the organist began to bang out the first hymn, she had no choice but to join the rest of the family at the font. Carla mouthed "Sorry!" as Xenia's christening gown caught on a button of her skirt and Natasha let out a yelp.

As the singing came to an end, Carla felt her breathing ease. Perhaps Seb wasn't coming after all. She didn't suppose it mattered so much if he didn't show- it wasn't as if there was a shortage of godparents. Carla gazed around the tiny church bedecked with winter roses cut just hours before from Natasha's amazing chess garden. Carla's own hellebores were never this pure a white - more like a sickly green. The Dowager Countess was a vision in head to toe Iris-coloured mink. Along with Natasha in her midnight velvet, the two women were as elegant and remote as the recumbent effigies on the tombs. The vicar handed a candle to one of Natasha's daughters, washed his hands in a little dish and was about to invite the godparents 'to reject Satan and all his practices' when the roof of the church began to vibrate. Even the smallest of the stained-glass windows began to rattle.

"Talk of the -" said Xavier puffing air through his cheeks. The low throttle of a helicopter grew to a deafening crescendo before the engine suddenly cut out altogether. There were shouts from outside, and the sound of men running. Then a gust of wind as the massive oak door was heaved open. Fir cones, gravel and a dusting of snow heralded Seb's arrival, and then there was Seb himself, stamping his boots before jogging down the aisle, his cashmere coat flapping behind him like a cloak.

He beamed utterly unperturbed by the dowager's frigid stare, by the other godparents, Natasha or even a now screaming Xenia who'd been disturbed by the church door slamming. Only the twins had perked up with the commotion.
"Polo," smiled Seb happily by way of an excuse adding the prefix "winter" as if this would somehow exonerate him. Natasha scowled, turning away from him. Carla noted the hundreds of tiny covered buttons marching down her spine.

"Smile!" said the photographer.

And they all did - except that Carla's, which had begun as a broad grin, turned to a perfect 'o' as Seb squeezing in beside her, hugged her to him and pinched her bottom.

Natasha had invited half the village for a glass of champagne to wet the baby's head, and neighbours came and went throughout the afternoon. Dogs ran freely through the reception rooms and children high on E numbers scampered after them. Carla was aware of Seb in the large drawing-room as though they were the only two people left in the universe, well almost the only two. The twins made periodic interruptions to ask when they were leaving.

"We can't until after lunch," said Carla firmly.

"But it *is* after lunch!" Sophie retorted. "It's practically night outside!"

Her fascinator had lost most of its feathers, and she'd taken off her shoes. Sophie was right, lunch should have been over hours ago, but Carla knew Natasha wanted to eat by candlelight and they weren't going to be sitting down until the last of the neighbours had gone home. Truth to tell, Carla didn't mind. She didn't want to leave just yet, not while there was a chance of speaking to Seb. The other godmother gave a pretty speech, the other godfather promised support in the years to come, Seb promised to lead Xenia astray which predictably went down badly with the dowager and Carla muttered something about a Catholic influence which went down badly with the vicar.

"Don't think we've quite made the cut, do you?" whispered Seb in her ear.

Carla smirked. "Xenia will thank us when she's older. Besides, I couldn't care less," and to her amazement, she who'd always been so worried about what people thought, realised that she really didn't.

Seb was about to say something else when a recently divorced neighbour touched his arm. Carla knew Helene from when the twins were small. Helene with an 'e' never an 'a'. For a time, Sophie and her daughter had been best friends. Helene was a tall Norwegian ex-model. Perennially tanned, she'd always been very sexy with a low, seductive voice. When she left her husband, she'd also sparked a collective shiver by announcing ominously that she'd had affairs with lots of married men in Wiltshire. Sophie sometimes wondered if Angus was one of them. Dressed in a figure-hugging dress, her tanned cleavage was now faintly wrinkled, but she was still attractive with colouring not unlike Seb's. Maybe, he was half Norwegian too.

"Please tell me," she said sweetly, ignoring Carla, "Why *do* they change ends in polo?"

"Yes, do explain it please," said Carla mimicking her friend's breathless intonation and noticing how Seb automatically sucked in his cheekbones to give them both the full benefit of his penetrating blue eyes. By the time Seb had finished explaining the rules of the game - the fact that changing ends after each goal helped to equalise any ground or weather advantages - that a bell is rung after every 7 minutes, Helene had downed another three glasses. It was when she went off to find a fourth, that Carla made a face.

"She did ask," he said, setting aside his own glass and leaning nonchalantly on the marble mantlepiece, one leg resting on the hearth. In the half-light, his white shirt glowed against his dark skin.

"Oh, do tell me more," said Carla breathlessly sounding like Helene but only because desire had suddenly pooled in her belly. "Really?"

"No."

He smiled, eyes twinkling. "Bad girl."

"Had I known how you were going to behave," said Natasha sailing past. "I'd have put you two in the kitchen with the staff! Come on, I'm starving!".

Seb raised his eyebrows. "Uh oh, I don't think her ladyship was joking either."

Natasha settled herself at the head of the table, a now quieter Xenia on her lap, her beautiful christening robes carefully arranged around her. Mother and child looked like something out of a Sargent painting all froth and silk taffeta. The candle lit dining room was magical; light bounced off the many surfaces, from the crystal pear drops of the chandelier to the glasses and decanters. Pink champagne shimmered in rose gold buckets of ice. Trumeau mirrors reflected silver bowls stuffed to overflowing with tuberoses and boughs of evergreen. The scent of both was intoxicating. Carla closed her eyes, transported to another time, where there was no past and no future, where she could start anew.

"Ready for this?" Seb whispered, guiding Carla to her place. She was aware of the firmness of his touch, his smell - a clean white linen smell - a familiarity that made her want to lean her head against him. For a moment, he lingered behind her, his hands on either side of her as if steadying her for what was to come. Whatever it was, it was too long for Natasha's liking. Her glare made him circle the table ostentatiously. He knew he'd been seated opposite Carla and returned Natasha's disapproving look with a gleeful smile.

But although he was careful to talk to the guests on either side of him, Carla was painfully aware of him, aware of every gesture, every inflexion, the way he would suddenly look at her across the table, catching her unawares so that flustered, she would look away. Most of all, she was conscious of his restlessness, his taut frame too large for the Sheraton chairs. He ate very little, fiddling with his cutlery throughout the meal. Carla couldn't eat either, a little bit tipsy, a great deal excited. For the first time ever, or so it felt, she was aware of the physicality of a man, in the holding her breath kind of way, in the tension throughout her body kind of way, in an all-consuming, lustful kind of way. Perhaps it was all his talk of snow polo that the analogy sprang to mind. It felt as though she'd been pushed onto a bobsled that she'd never asked to get on in the first place, and was now hurtling along a steep, icy groove from which there was no escape. She could neither stop nor turn back.

"There's a wall around you," he'd said after the cake had been passed around - well to everyone but Seb and Carla. "You don't deserve any," said Natasha moving behind the guests floating a large platter above their heads. Slices of fruitcake with more marzipan. "At least not yet - far too naughty. The pair of you." Seb made a face that made Carla giggle.

"Is this made from a tier of your wedding cake?" Helene asked. "You're supposed to do that in England, aren't you?"

"No," said Natasha. "Xavier and I ate that. We thought we couldn't have children, so we didn't think there was any point in saving it."

"Well, that really worked," joked someone else.

"You haven't said anything," said Seb across the table, for her alone.

"What?" blinked Carla still thinking of the bobsled, her heart hammering in her chest, feeling more alive than she had ever felt in her entire life. And more terrified.

"A wall," said Seb making a twirling gesture with his hand. "You have a wall around you."

"No, I don't," said Carla. "There's no wall around me."

Seb wasn't even looking at her when he replied. "Then prove it."

Nor she at him. She didn't dare. *Just let me…*

"How?"

His whole head moved owl-like and when his eyes locked with hers she knew the sledge had crashed. "Have lunch with me."

And so, she had, but not then, not for a long time. At first, Seb only called, but he had every day, and at the same time and on the landline. The house that was so quiet and still came to life then, the air crackling with palpable excitement, with the anticipation, the rush to be back from Sophie's school run, to be on time. But he never failed. And she talked. Ignored for so many years, she talked and talked, and he listened. Afterwards, the house was warm and snug. Carla ran around lighting fires, lugging in wood from the sheds, foraging for kindle, baking Sophie cakes for tea, lighting candles for their kitchen suppers when it was just the two of them. Tom was away at school and Sophie, if she wasn't riding her pony, was at home with Carla. But if Seb by now, knew just about everything there was to know about Carla, Carla still knew almost nothing about Seb. He had only recently moved to London and he played polo most days. He had never married but as to why he had remained single remained a mystery.

"Never met the right woman," he'd said glibly. "Not true" he corrected once when he let slip his guard. "I did, but she died. It's all right," he'd said not quickly but in a measured way to reassure her. "It was a long time ago. I'm not damaged, don't think that." Carla didn't think that, but she did believe that the girl/woman would be a hard act to follow. "So, what do you want?" He'd asked and not in the ''appiness' way. He'd put on a French accent mimicking the oft-quoted Mme. de Gaulle.

What *did* she want? Sobriety for Angus would always be top of her list. But for herself? She realised that she was now separating herself from her husband; that she no longer considered Angus to be part of her 'we'. *You*, she wanted to say. *I want you.*

And still, the lunch that he proposed, and she'd not exactly refused but hadn't committed to either, didn't happen. She continued to live her life quietly in the country looking after Sophie during the week then both children at the weekend when Tom came home from school. But the problems that seemed insurmountable when Angus first left for Russia, were less daunting when she could discuss them with Seb. She phoned him when she had a flat tyre, when the Aga ran out of oil, when two crows came down the chimney, and broke her Meissen plates - actually they broke one and then came back for the other. She phoned him when she discovered poachers on her land wringing the neck of a pheasant in front of an hysterical Sophie, and one policeman arrived on a bicycle too nervous about giving chase to 'lads with knives.' She phoned him when the boiler broke down, when one of Sophie's pet rabbits escaped and especially when she couldn't sleep one night after watching a mystery drama. She phoned to ask his opinion on a brocade jacket that she'd seen in a local designer shop.

"What did you do before you married?" He'd asked one night when he'd taken longer than usual to answer before she noticed the time.

"Oh, sorry, were you sleeping?"

"No, I never sleep much before 4 a.m."

"4?" She'd been shocked. "But that's no time at all!"

He gave a virtual shrug. "Too pumped up after playing."

"But it's not the season?" She knew enough now not to ask silly questions.

"No, but I play arena all year round - less likely to die." He'd said it glibly. "And you? What did you do? Before you married Angus?"

What indeed? Her working life, such as it was, felt so long ago. She'd read History at university, married Angus the day she finished her finals and had the twins soon after. During the early months of her pregnancy, and then again after the twins started school, but before they'd moved to the country, she'd worked as a translator for United Distillers at their head office in Hammersmith. She'd loved that job.

"What kind of things did you translate?" Seb had wanted to know.

It was her turn to shrug virtually. "Not much really - telegrams mostly. Although there was the occasional holdup - even a kidnapping once."

"No?"

"Yes!"

"And that's what you enjoyed?"

She'd nodded into the phone.

"More than History?"

"That was just a degree although I love visiting historic houses, does that count?"

"No."

"So how about going back to work? Doing something with your languages? Spanish right?"

"I do work. I told you - translation for pharmaceutical companies."

"That sounds lonely."

"It isn't really."

"Don't you want to be out and about working with people?"

The thought terrified her. "But I have the twins. One boards, the other's at school. This way, I can fit my work around them." She could think of a dozen reasons why she didn't want to commit to more, but none of them was persuasive when she said them out loud to Seb.

"Right," he'd said then. "We'll discuss it next week. Monday. Lunch, 12.30 Oriols. I'll meet you there."

Carla had had a whole week in which to prepare. She didn't call Seb at all during that time, nor he her. For once, she didn't need his opinion on anything. This was up to her. She knew he was waiting, that there was no more to be decided. Except for her clothes. She tried on different combinations: sleek leather jackets with floaty dresses, the clean silhouette of a blazer and a white shirt, wool skirts with a bolero and big buttons. In the end, it was too cold to wear anything but a taupe sheepskin coat with chocolate suede knee-high boots over a cashmere shift. Trembling with nerves - it was somehow less threatening to have a friendship with someone over the phone than in real life - she'd headed for London. By the time she arrived at Waterloo, it had begun to snow, a light sheen that covered everything in a delicate, lethal layer. She shivered with terror at the idea of seeing Seb again and several times thought about cancelling. But the bustle of the station and the sheer adrenaline of the city was contagious, and she'd felt its energy with fresh excitement.

But Carla hesitated again by the taxi rank. She didn't want to arrive too early, didn't want to be *seen* arriving if Seb were waiting outside the restaurant. Carla actually enjoyed the anonymity of the tube, so after a few minutes, she left the queue. Feeling the rush of air as she descended into the bowels of the underground, Carla alternated between feeling gloriously alive to utterly appalled and terrified. Going to meet Seb was the most dangerous thing she'd ever considered. Playing for time, Carla decided to alight at Knightsbridge rather than the closer stop of Sloane Square and walk the remaining distance. Her heart thumping uncomfortably, she tried to regulate her breathing, inhaling gulps of cold air.

For a few moments, she stood at the top end of Sloane Street, contemplating its swish designer stores and pretty street lamps. Shoppers strolled leisurely oblivious of the increasing snowfall. Wafts of expensive perfume hung in the air long after the men and women had passed by. The rich moved

differently thought Carla, they never hurried anywhere.
Towards the bottom end of the street were communal
gardens where residents played tennis in warmer weather.
There was still time to turn back, Carla told herself. This was
such an unwise move. She was married. Married women
absolutely did not have lunch with single men, fellow
godparent or not.

But the stronger, more compelling argument was that she
was saving herself for a man who didn't want her as opposed
to one that did. Would this be the moment she regretted for
the rest of her life if she *didn't* go to meet Seb? Was this that
chance of happiness a second time around that *wouldn't* come
around again? It was snowing hard now, shoppers sank into
chauffeur-driven cars or flagged down taxis disappearing
into warm interiors. The light from the square was pink and
orange as Carla hurried on. Something more powerful than
her reason or will propelled her towards a different destiny,
and she knew nothing short of an accident could stop her
now.

And then, one almost had. As she stepped onto the zebra
crossing in front of the Cadogan Hall, a Mercedes passed
within inches of her. Carla jumped back horrified by her
momentary inattention. She might have escaped with her life,
but the heel of her Azagury boot snapped in two. Maybe it
was a sign, thought Carla. Her heel had also broken the night
of the pre-Christening dinner. But unlike that time, she
couldn't run upstairs and change. She couldn't run anywhere
as it happened. Glancing up, at that moment, heel in hand she
saw Seb. He was standing on the corner of Eaton Square,
hands thrust deep into the pockets of his Loro Piana coat. The
khaki suede of its collar pulled up against his ears made his
face appear even more tanned. Her heart gave a lurch and she
knew then that it was too late. What would be was already

decided and had been the moment he touched the scar on her forehead, the moment Natasha asked her to be Xenia's godmother, the moment he suggested there was a wall around her. The moment he asked her if she was happily married. Snow melted on her hair, settled on the tip of her nose, on her lips.

His expression was quizzical, but as she limped towards him, he broke into a grin. "What on earth?"

She hesitated not at all when he opened his arms wide. As if there was no one to see them, as if they were the only two people in the world, with no past, no complications, she laid her head against his chest, to be wrapped up completely in his arms and the lapel of his coat. Against the smell of suede and cashmere and linen, she closed her eyes, welcoming his unfamiliarity, his virility, his assuredness, knowing she was seen at last.

14

For a moment, Carla's heart stood still. *Please God, no ... please. Anything,* she prayed. *Why aren't you listening? I said I'd do anything!* There was a police bicycle propped against the side of the house but the hall, when she entered, was in darkness. No one appeared to be home - no tell-tale coats or shoes by the door - the shoes that Seb and Alfie kicked off when they went in - the shoes that either slammed against her beautiful desk or chipped the skirting board. She'd never mind again, nor retrieve them making that tutting sound. She was completely out of breath and catching sight of herself in the full-length hall mirror, not at all surprised that the widow/woman had been reluctant to talk to her. She looked as if she'd been living on the streets herself.

Her shins were caked with dried blood and along the way, her hair had collected a few twigs, even the delicate strands of a spider's web. Her shirt had ripped further - in fact, one sleeve was almost hanging off completely. Her whole body began to shake uncontrollably. And then she heard men's voices coming from the back, but whether, from her own garden or a neighbour's, she couldn't tell. She edged slowly down the whole length of the house, propelled robotically towards the voices. The French doors were open, and a policeman moved into sight, standing under the cherry tree. He stood the requisite two metres from Seb and wore a mask and rubber gloves.

At the sight of him, Carla froze, unable to take another step forward, unable to speak. She felt a prickly sweat creep up the back of her neck. Swirls of blackness swam before her eyes, then receded then moved closer, ever more enveloping.

Just when she thought the moment had passed, the cloud descended again, this time wiping out her sight. She put out a hand to stop herself falling, teetering headlong into the abyss. Too exhausted to fight any more, she threw up her arms as though jumping into water, surrendering herself willingly to the prospect of oblivion.

"Mrs. Cave?"

"Carla!"

"*Mummy!*"

In that order, the voices pierced her subconscious. Slowly, she opened her eyes or could see, she wasn't sure which - uncertain as to whether she'd imagined them, willed the last one. But the pressure of Alfie's arms around her waist, his hot face pressed against her chest, his boy smell she clung to, because even if he wasn't real, she would savour the memory forever.

She heard the policeman reassure Seb, who was thanking him for his trouble - for wasting his time - *'No, trust me this is the result we'd want.'* There were 'stay safes' all around, the unfamiliar sound of a two-way radio, the thud of the man's boots, and finally, the slamming of the front door. That wasn't imagined - and still, Alfie remained, arms wrapped around her.

Oh!" said Carla at last because he was real, "Oh, my precious! I'm so sorry! I'm so sorry!"

And then Seb's arms were around them both, and she remembered that first time, when she'd limped towards him, and he'd enveloped her in all of him. Her head now as then, was crushed against his chest, Alfie's against hers. There was no *'Wash your hands!'* this time. There was only that moment together, the three of them. Whatever doubts she'd had, were smothered in the closeness of their embrace. She felt that she had been saved, pulled from the brink of something terrible. She'd come within a whisker of tragedy. It was time, at last, to draw a line over the past and to survive this present; not just survive - she'd been doing that barely, but to do it well. To live now.

The remains of the picnic Seb had bought for them was spread out on the teak table under the cherry tree.

"Come on, Mum," said Alfie, drawing away from her. "It's OK. Nothing bad happened. Let's have some lunch."

Carla wiped her face with the sleeve of her torn shirt.

"Wait," said Seb. "No, not you -" he said to their son with a smile. "Alfie you can go down to the cellar and fetch us a bottle of rosé. It looks like the one I bought for our picnic - he pointed to a bottle resting on the counter. "That one'll be too warm now. Fetch a cold one from the cellar and take it outside." He turned back to his wife. "Carla."

It wasn't a question. Seb remained standing close to her as Alfie had run past them and down the stairs.

"Wh-what happened?" she began. "Where did you find Alfie?"

Seb held her face in both hands, pressing his lips lightly to hers. "Sh!" he began. "I'll - *we'll* tell you all about it later." He smoothed her hair. "We'll get through this," he said gently after a while. "I'm sorry for what happened ... before. You know I am. And I also know that what you're going through now has everything to do with then. I love you," he finished simply. "All I can do is keep loving you until one day you really forgive me. I mean with all your heart not just because of Alfie, not just going through the motions but because you forgive *me*. I want things to work."

Suddenly the spinning stopped, the constant noise in her head of recent years, kept at its own particular pitch by guilt and self-doubt, calmed and was still.

"And I'm sorry too," she said. "I'm sorry too."

15

"Everything OK?" said Seb a few mornings later. Since the river 'episode' as they now referred to it, Carla had resolved to change. It was part of the promise she'd made to herself if Alfie was found safe and sound and she was determined to keep her secret pact. She'd begun by cleaning the house from top to bottom. She'd stripped beds, washed bedlinen, disinfected bathrooms, picked flowers from the cutting garden and purchased others from M&S where, after a few weeks of scarcity, its stock was back to pre-virus levels. (Not that she'd noticed in her past lethargy). She'd even tackled Alfie's hair and was quite pleased with the results. Her own was more problematic, but she had ordered some hair dye online and would get Seb to help her apply it when it arrived. Today, it was her closet's turn, and Carla sat in the middle of the floor in her dressing room, sorting through piles of clothes. Her best designer dresses were ready for re-sale in their garment protectors. Other outfits she never wore were in plastic bags. Stacks of handbags and shoes were still in their original boxes. "It's…" he glanced at his phone. "6.30 a.m. - are you sure you're OK?"

"Yes," she chirped. "Absolutely fine."

Seb crossed his arms, leaning against the door jam.

"Good, good. Er… it's just early, that's all. Are we supposed to be somewhere later?"

He was hesitant with the last bit. They were both supremely careful not to offend each other.

"Well, Alfie and I have an appointment at 9 a.m.," she said, wrapping a pink cashmere jumper in tissue paper. She slipped a couple of moth balls between the folds. Moths had been an unwelcome sitting tenant when they moved in. "But I want to pack up this lot before then."

Seb frowned. "I don't understand. You love your clothes."

Carla patted a tan Hermès Birkin. "Yup - I do - *did*," she corrected. "I just don't need this kind of thing anymore." She looked around the room. "I don't wear half these clothes as it is. To be honest, I don't know if I ever will. Not any time soon. Do you realise that this little baby could probably match Captain Tom's contribution?"

Seb didn't hesitate this time. "Sell it," he said.

Carla looked sheepish.

"Sometimes I wonder at myself."

Seb knew better than to respond to the 'sometimes.'

"Some of this is brand new," she said catching his look and delving into a shoe box before he had time to say anything. She prized out a satin Manolo mule, trimmed in mink. A tiny diamanté clasp nestled in its fur. She held it at arm's length admiring the exquisite craftsmanship. "I mean, where on earth did I think I'd wear this?"

"Maybe for the life we used to lead?"

Seb looked pensive. There was a time when they'd flown to parties in private jets, spent summers gliding from Capri to Syracuse on a yacht, watched Seb play winter polo in Klosters. Before Alfie's birth and when he was tiny, they'd spent the whole month of January in St. Barths.

"You don't miss the Bahamas?"

Seb had that uncanny way of reading her mind.

Carla's eyes widened. "You mean Lifeless Cay?"

He looked surprised. "Is that what you thought of Lyford?"

Carla looked sheepish.

"Not even a bit?"

"Not even a bit."

"And these?"

Seb picked up a pair of sky-high Louboutins. The lipstick red soles were pristine.

"Those!" Carla scoffed. "Have honestly got to be the most uncomfortable shoes I've ever owned! My feet have PTSD just looking at them. I think I can only wear them lying down."

Seb's eyes twinkled. "Now, there's a thought."

"Actually, we've never worn shoes, less have we? The floors are so lovely and toastie we don't need to, and I certainly don't need heels for what I'm planning to do." She shook her head in disbelief. "I can't believe any of this once meant something."

Seb placed the shoes back on the 'to sell' pile. "But it might again one day. Lockdown has to end. Won't you regret getting rid of all this? You always do, you know."

There had been times in the past when in a spurt of generosity, she'd given away items of clothing and then regretted it. Now she meant business. "Nope," she picked up a roll of masking tape. "I'm selling this lot - the proceeds are going to the Hampshire Air Ambulance. I'm going to use the rest to make masks out of and/or bags to put scrubs in -"

"And *this*?" Seb was incredulous. "Please don't tell me this is the luggage with the carbon steel bearings *and* aircraft-grade aluminium handles?"

Carla grinned. "The very same. Well, we can't travel anywhere, can we? And *mi amor*, I'm delighted that this gear *is* made of vegan leather - the company is recycling its bags to make masks and gloves and other protective gear." She packaged the carry-on into its original box. Carla was meticulous at keeping an item's original packaging. She tore off a strip of masking tape with her teeth. "And talking of aircraft," she said. "Did you see where Avianca has gone bust? Who would have thought it?"

Seb shook his head. "Who'd have thought any of it?" He straightened. "Come here," he whispered.

"What do you think? Silk Pucci face mask or bag for dirty PPE?"

In a swift move, he'd pulled her to her feet. "I think neither Mrs. Cave," he said. "I think the place for you at this precise moment is -"

She leant into him. "Oh, OK then," she said with a smile. "But only because it's so early."

An hour or so later, Carla made the bed taking real pleasure in shaking out the embroidered linen sheets, smoothing the French quilt and plumping up the pretty cushions in their Pierre Frey fabric. The whole bedroom smelt of orange and bergamot and was bathed in a lemony meringue light. She showered, washed her hair and tied back her hair before putting on her gym gear.

"You," she said to Seb as they stood together at the bottom of Alfie's attic stairs.

"No, you," he said.

"Really, you. I wouldn't deny you the pleasure!"

Seb touched her shoulder lightly.

"OK, but your turn next time."

Carla followed him up the narrow stairs. Seb had to duck before he reached the top. She kicked the beanbags out of the way and switched on the TV while Seb knocked on the door of Alfie's bedroom. She'd cleaned up in here too - no easy task. Carla had been shocked to find rotting apple cores, pizza boxes under armchairs, Tango cans, sweet wrappers, half-eaten biscuits - all evidence of the many takeaways Seb had ordered in the weeks of her 'sabbatical' from family life. The lovely attic room with its Turkish rugs and Regency desk was dusty and grimy. Clearing out all the debris had been sobering. Through the smallest window, along a skyline of tiled sloping roofs, the Cathedral remained undiminished, tranquil and serene though its bells were silent.

"I'm not getting up now!" she could hear Alfie protesting.

"Oh, yes, you are big guy," Seb cajoled. "Joe Wicks is waiting!"

As if on cue, she flicked a switch and the exuberant image of the nation's number one fitness coach bounced across the screen. Unlike hers, his hair looked silky and uniformly coloured. Seb mouthed 'Good luck!" before disappearing downstairs again.

"We're doing this together!" she said chirpily although she was soon panting, aching and (inwardly) swearing.

"And *then* I'm resting," said Alfie sulkily plopping down on one of the bean bags.

"Uh uh," said Carla performing jumping jacks. She pulled her son to his feet as she jumped. He felt more substantial than he had a few months ago. In the background, Joe Wicks reeled off the names of the thousands of viewers tuning in from across the world. *"And a shout out from… Moscow!"* There was no denying the man's enthusiasm.

"And *then*, we're home schooling." Carla's announcement was met with less. I thought we'd start with English. I thought we could read Daniel Dafoe's *Journal of the Plague Year* together."

Alfie stopped jumping.

"You're joking."

"Not in the slightest. I also thought you could start a diary of your own. Keep exercising. We're not done."

"A *diary*! Why? None of my friends is."

"It's hard to know what your friends are doing," said Carla grunting as Wicks began a kind of 'spider' move. She felt faintly ridiculous, throwing out a pretend web by unfurling her hand. Alfie had slumped back down the minute she'd mentioned 'reading' and was now looking at YouTube clips. "Besides, one day you'll look back on this time. Someone will ask you how you spent lockdown. I want you to be proud of yourself. Come on, it's a challenge. It's good for you - therapeutic even."

Joe Wicks kangarooed across the screen, flicking back his long curly locks. No lockdown body on this man.

"Is that a *cast*?" Seb's head and shoulders appeared at the top of the attic stairs. He sounded delighted. He frowned at his son. "Big guy, what are you doing?"

Alfie looked up briefly. "Having a break. Yeah, he fell off his bike and broke a bone in his hand."

"Wow!" said Carla breathing hard. "I didn't even notice. I'm impressed he can still do all that. Would even *want* to! And look that good."

"Mmmn," said Seb frowning, sizing up the man's six-pack clearly visible under his skin-tight t-shirt. "A bit girlie, if you know what I mean."

"He has a daughter, Dad," said Alfie in disgust.

By 10 a.m. she and Alfie were at the kitchen table. Carla slid her Mac towards him so that they could share the screen. She'd googled everything vaguely 'plaguey'. Sales of Camus' *La Peste* had gone from a couple of hundred the year before, to over a thousand in one week alone.

"So, let's start," she said flipping open the cover of her kindle. She'd downloaded a pile of books from the internet. "I'm going to read a little bit aloud every day - just a little bit and then you can write your own entry."

Alfie was surprisingly compliant although when she peeked over his shoulder, his pages seemed to cover what he'd had for dinner and listing the computer games he was being allowed to play. At lunch, they went on virtual gallery tours and listened to TED Talks on famous painters. They started with Van Gogh. Alfie wept when she played him Don Mclean's *Vincent*.

"Going well then?" said Seb coming into the kitchen noticing the tears.

"Can I play my game now?" said Alfie.

"Sure, big guy," said Seb sending Carla a *It's tough for the poor kid* kind of look, but Carla had other ideas. *Yeah, and my heart bleeds* hers shot back.

"Grab your hoodie," she said, getting up from the table to put her coffee mug in the dishwasher and shut down her screen.

"Not another walk!" groaned Alfie.

"Kind of - but one with purpose." Carla gave Seb a hug as she passed by him. She took her raincoat from the rack in the hall. "You might want to get yours too," she added in answer to his questioning look. "I've signed us all up. Don't laugh but we're going to help out with deliveries for the KPO. On foot. And we can split up, so it's faster. If Captain - sorry, *Colonel* Tom can do it, so can we!"

"Yeah, but he's getting a knighthood for his trouble," said Alfie grumpily.

Carla feigned shock. "And I'm *sure* it never occurred to him when he started walking around his garden." She grabbed keys, no handbag - she didn't own one that wasn't a designer statement and completely inappropriate for doing errands. "Bring your skateboard - you'll be finished in no time."

Seb took his Guards' Polo windcheater from the peg beside

hers.

"What?"

He shook his head. "You, me, us." His eyes flicked over her body, taking in her plimsolls (purchased on eBay for £6) and jeans, a far cry from her usual designer get up. "Do you remember when we first met?"

"You were late and waltzed down the aisle like the caped crusader?"

Seb was pleased. "Well yes, now that you mention it, but no, I meant in general. We were both so... so finickity."

"There was a lot of flouncing."

"There still is sometimes."

"Yes."

"I meant we were quite precious - in terms of how we dressed - what we would and would not do."

It was Carla's turn to run her eyes over Seb. It was true he had always lived in jeans and blue cashmere sweaters, but once the jeans had been branded, the cashmere only the very finest. Now, both were lesser-known brands and although he still wore his Guards jacket, he'd long since given up polo - no more men in whites.

"Maybe we've grown up."

"Maybe, it's this Covid thing."

Carla nodded. "I think it's been a blessing," she said slowly. "For me, at least. I think it saved me. *Us*."

He took her hand in both of his, holding it steady before raising it to his lips. Still holding her hand, he opened the front door.

"Come on, boy!" he called to their son and together they walked down Canon Street, Alfie gliding on his skateboard ahead of them.

16

Early one morning, towards the end of May, after Boris made his 'big' announcement - the one that was even more confusing as to what people could and could not do, the one that inspired hundreds of more jokes and more memes (especially abroad) but implied that some restrictions had been lifted and people were still uncertain as to what those really were, the one that said that the government had changed its slogan from 'stay home' to 'stay alert', there was a knock on the door.

"I've brought my own disinfectant," said Tom grinning. Her older boy stood on the pavement waving a bottle of hand sanitiser, a rucksack over one shoulder. Carla hadn't seen Tom since lockdown began. Her heart caught in her throat and for a moment, not only could she not speak, but she actually thought she would burst into tears. She hadn't realised what a difference it would make seeing him in the flesh. They'd Zoomed, FaceTimed and spoken during the past months but it wasn't the same as seeing him standing there in front of her. The weekend before would have been his graduation, but he had still been called to the bar.

"Ah, but no touching!" he said, taking a step back. He looked pleased by Carla's reaction all the same. "Where's Alfie?"

"Here!" said Alfie bouncing into his arms. Clearly one rule for her... but she didn't mind. The boys adored each other. Tom hugged his younger brother although he was no longer a child - more of a lumpy youth having filled out since lockdown began. Carla glanced away, her once skinny baby was actually chubby.

"Come on in," she said, opening the door wide.

Tom shook his head.

"Actually, you're coming out."

Carla shifted her weight. She forgot she always needed to be one step ahead of the twins; there was something she was missing but she couldn't say what it was exactly. She was out of practice. It was a long time since she'd seen either of them together or separately.

"I-I don't understand."

But Tom was looking over her shoulder to Seb who'd appeared silently behind her.

"Ready?" said Tom.

"Just about," said Seb. He was dressed for the beach - a towel around his neck - his Akubra which always spelt days in the sun - not quite square on his head. He lifted a cool-box. "Ice-olation - spelt i-c-e - cocktails at the ready - or as good as. The means to make 'em anyway."

"Oh, very good," said Tom.

Seb gave a curt bow. The kind he'd practiced when he'd met the Queen. "Glad you appreciate the pun."

Carla shook her head. "Really not clear at all."

"You don't have to be, Mum." Tom turned to his little brother. "You got my text, right?"

"Yup," said Alfie smiling. "I've got the drone and the Frisbee and my swimmers."

"Good man," said his father. "But what about Mummy's - those are the important ones."

"Got those," said Alfie fishing out a pair of Carla's bikini bottoms from his pocket.

"And the top?" said Seb, amused.

"Oh, yeah," said Alfie. "I forgot girls need that bit."

Carla shook her head. "Will you please tell me what's going on?"

Tom gave his hand sanitiser a couple of pumps as Alfie lowered himself off him, meticulously wiping between the fingers.

"You tell her," he said. "I've got a postcode. We'll meet in the car park."

Seb almost pushed Carla out of the door.

"Hey - wait! Where are we going?"

"At least it's not *what* am I wearing!" said Seb.

"Wow," said Tom. "Mum really has changed!"

Carla shrugged, running her hands over her skimpy shorts. She felt better than she had in a long time. This was the real her.

Alfie handed her a battered sun hat and her sunglasses.

"You don't need anything Mummy. Anyway, it's a surprise!"

"Oh, well done!" said Seb.

"I kind of gathered," said Carla as they began walking towards where the car was parked in College Street.

"And it's legal," said Seb. "Well, it will be tomorrow - we're a day early. The weather's too good to miss."

Carla enjoyed the inquisitive looks of her neighbours as she traipsed behind her family barefoot. Gone were the days when she never looked anything less than immaculate before stepping out of the house.

"If Tom is here, then it must be," she said happily, although the fact that Sophie wasn't, took the edge off her joy. "You won't tell me where we're going?"

"No way!" said Alfie. "Except that -"

"Except nothing," Seb interrupted firmly. "There's nothing you need to know at this moment. All you have to do is get in the car and sit tight. We'll take care of the rest, right Alfie?"

"R-right," said Alfie uncertainly. Carla could tell he was bursting to tell her.

"Gosh," said Carla. "I don't think I've ever had a surprise planned for me."

"It wasn't really planned," said Alfie. "It just happened."

Seb shot Alfie another warning.

"Not another word," he said. "Zip it."

"But Daddy I -"

"No - you can have my phone. I don't trust you to keep quiet."

As if on cue, her own pinged. It was a while since she'd heard from Les Girls - the immediate urgency had slipped from their messages as they were absorbed by broader interests.

They discussed the hobbies keeping them going during lockdown, gardening tips on how to keep weeds at bay, on how to grow vegetables (Carla wished she'd paid more attention to that one - all the little seeds Alfie had planted in yoghurt pots had been burnt by the sun) and the challenge of motivating teenagers now that they weren't working towards exams.

Southampton is trialling a vaccine in the over 70s

Dentists are re-opening

Non-essential shops from 15th June!

No new cases in Suffolk

Or Shropshire

Or Oxford

"I think the country has decided time's up," said Carla as they left the town centre. The city was heaving. The once deserted green in front of the Cathedral was packed with people sitting on the grass, playing games or drinking coffee from one of the two places offering takeaway. The only pub on the square was also offering beer in plastic glasses, the queue waiting to purchase beverages extending to the high street. Ice cream vendors were making a brisk trade and everywhere, bicycles weaved in and out of the crowds. No one was waiting for the official 1st of June ease up on lockdown. The Queen's message of hope and the promise that her subjects would 'meet again' was here. And although shops were still closed it felt kind of normal, it felt good.

"Dorset?" said Carla as they sped south.

"Maybe," said Seb.

"Yes, it's Dorset!" piped up, Alfie. "Well, not exactly Dorset - it's-"

"No more!" warned Seb.

"The sea!" exclaimed Carla in delight. "You had me confused for a moment." They had travelled on back roads ignoring the signs to Lymington and Highcliffe Castle to emerge further down the headland. Surprisingly, given the lovely weather they'd come across very few cars heading for the seaside. The car park was virtually empty.

"Look, coffee!" said Carla spying a popup kiosk. "They're actually selling coffee! It'll be my first since lockdown began." Her eyes were shining. If she'd been offered champagne, she couldn't have been more thrilled.

Seb parked and began unloading. He looped beach bags over Alfie's shoulder and slapped a couple more hats on top of his Akubra while he carried the picnic. Carla went on ahead to buy a cappuccino and sipped it happily as they walked down the steep path to the beach, stopping for a moment to close her eyes and breathe in the hot air, the smell of the sea, the tang of salt.

"There he is!" said Seb waving. She opened her eyes slowly, squinting in the bright light. The sunglasses Alfie had sweetly thought to bring her, were a pair she'd bought when she was about eighteen from Top Shop in Oxford Street. They still looked pretty cool. They had large white, fifties-style frames and dark lenses but the glass itself was scratched and there was a star-shaped chip in the right-hand corner. Tom was already settled in a sheltered area against some rocks. Above him, the gulls screeched and swooped low.

Slowly, Carla felt herself relax, the tension, fear and yes shock of the past months, gradually easing from her body. Because it had been a shock - this pandemic - the way their lives had suddenly changed so dramatically. It had been a kind of trauma, and while on the whole, it had been a good thing for her and Seb, it had been much more challenging for Alfie. She wouldn't wish it on anyone. There was grit between her bare toes, as she picked her way gingerly over the pebbles until they found purchase once again on a sandy plain. Alfie ran on ahead to meet his brother. Seb walked with his hand on the nape of Carla's neck, balancing the cool box under one arm.

"Thank you," she said simply.

"It's not over yet," he said. "There's more."

She looked up expectantly, but he shook his head.

"This is heaven," she said.

"It's not St. Tropez," he said.

"Much nicer."

And she meant it.

The biggest surprise hadn't been coffee or the sea or leaving the city for the first time in months - they who were used to leaving the *country* more often than that. No, it had been the arrival of Sophie and Ed. She'd spied Ed's tall frame halfway down the beach identifying him, before she realised that the slight, beautiful girl in the pretty white dress beside him was Sophie. This time, the sob that caught in her throat gave way to proper tears. She'd glanced at Tom who smiled warmly and Seb who went forward to greet them. There was no need to say anything. Carla held out her arms, her heart; terrified that Sophie would ignore her. But she didn't.

Carla wondered at this ache of motherhood. It wasn't enough to love, love in itself wasn't an *excuse* for the damage caused, it was an ongoing state, a continuum. Once a mother had children, she was marked. No happiness would ever be complete without theirs. Each child was equally precious, and their happiness essential to Carla's own. It was something neither Seb nor Carla had fully understood when they'd met all those years before, so caught up as they'd been in their own growing up. But now, as she held Sophie, her delicate, angel bones so fragile under her hands, she only wanted to keep her safe, to be given a second chance.

"What's for lunch?" Alfie plopped down on a towel, sprinkling sand in all directions.

"Agh!" exclaimed Sophie loudly wiping her eyes. "Be careful!"

"Smoked salmon, chicken legs, cold roast beef," said Seb, "strawberries and meringues for dessert - oh and sourdough bread." He held out an urchin-shaped mass. Alfie made a face.

"*That's* sourdough bread? It doesn't look anything like the pics on Insta."

Seb considered the knobbly mound. "Yes, well," he said. "But we've got lashings of ginger beer!"

"Who even *says* that anymore?" said Tom.

Seb and Carla exchanged a look. They did - Colonials like them who'd grown up on Enid Blyton.

Afterwards, the twins and Ed played cricket with Alfie.

"You should swim," said Seb as Carla lay basking

contentedly in the sun. It was the first time she'd ever sunbathed by the sea in England. But then they were usually abroad at this time of year. She felt drowsy with happiness. To have her three children was joy itself. To have Sophie with her, was a particular blessing.

"I will," she said, not moving.

"Go on!" encouraged Seb.

"Mummy's going in!" yelled Alfie.

"Go, Mum!" yelled the twins.

Carla grimaced. Nothing for it. She got up dusting sand off her bottom.

"Are you coming?" she asked Seb.

"Nope. Just wanted your towel."

"Oh, you toad!" she said, but she was up now. She shaded her eyes. The 'children' were happily playing. She smiled to herself. Technically, Alfie was the only 'child.' Tom was a barrister about to 'eat dinners' - that extraordinary practice peculiar to the English - and Sophie was an accountant. Carla had already had the twins by the time she was Sophie's age. She cast a glance down the beach. People of all ages were lapping up the sun - youngsters built sandcastles, teenagers kicked a ball, older couples walked hand in hand. There was a general sense of liberation and a gentleness that she didn't remember from even a few months ago; people smiled more readily.

Carla made her way carefully to the water's edge. Sand gave way to pebbles and large jagged rocks. She'd never swum in the Solent before and had a moment's trepidation when she wondered what lay beneath. She glanced around her. Enough swimmers were enjoying the water to reassure her. *Man up*, she told herself. It wasn't as if this was the Indian Ocean or South Pacific with the ever-present threat of shark attacks. The sea itself was opaque and so cold it numbed her lower limbs while above the surface, her skin tingled with the blistering heat of the sun. If she could venture deeper than her waist, then it would be easy. She splashed her chest and shoulders, salt and sand sliding off her skin. And then, taking a deep breath, she plunged to the bottom, pushing through the cold, metallic water, with strong even strokes. Above her secret silent world, silver and pewter beams of sunlight, blunted the tips of the waves.

Despite the air temperature, there was no gold or red or orange as in the Mediterranean. Here, everything was anthracite and deep blue, but no less beautiful. Carla swam horizontally towards the cliffs at the other end of the cove. An array of striped awnings blew jauntily from tiny beach huts. She was becoming accustomed to the cold now, and it was invigorating. The more she swam, the more powerful she became, garnering strength with every stroke. It felt as though she would never tire. It was only when she reached Mudeford, that she turned back so that she was swimming in view of the Isle of Wight.

Carla had swum in rivers and lakes and oceans all over the world. She still remembered the sheer force of the waves in Tulum, the stupor of the Arabian Sea and the balminess of the Caribbean. But no swim was as refreshing, or as cleansing, or as memorable, as that swim was that day. In the absence of boats and planes, the ha-ha-ha of seagulls was all the more achingly acute. She lay on her back allowing herself to float, tossed gently on the indrawn tide.

On the beach, the figures of her family came together, separated and came together again. As they would in life, going forward. There would be moments of harmony, others when, for whatever reason, they would be torn apart. This time, Carla was not afraid. Love of them would see her through. In the end, it was all that mattered. Sophie raised her arm and Carla waved back, holding on to that moment for as long as she could. Soon, but not quite yet, she would join them. She would approach shivering, and Seb would wrap her in a towel, his arms providing most of its warmth. Tom would open some wine, Ed would kick a ball to Alfie, and Carla would sit on the sand huddled close to the twins.

And they would stay that way until it was time to go home.

ABOUT THE AUTHOR

Susana Cory-Wright was born in Canada and grew up in Europe. After graduating with a degree in Modern Languages, she worked as a translator for pharmaceutical companies before embarking on a PhD in English. Her thesis formed the basis for her biography *Maud Beerbohm Tree, Lady of the Stage,* which was published by Legenda in 2018. She is the author of *The Catalan House* and *The London Wife*. She lives in Hampshire with her husband and young son.

Printed in Poland
by Amazon Fulfillment
Poland Sp. z o.o., Wrocław

62263263R00141